THE GREETER

THE GREETER

The Case of the
Missing Sweet Potato

Mary Ellen Cooper

HARBOR
HOUSE

Augusta

THE GREETER
THE CASE OF THE MISSING SWEET POTATO
By Mary Ellen Cooper
A Harbor House Book/2005

Copyright 2005 by Mary Ellen Cooper

For information address:
HARBOR HOUSE
111 TENTH STREET
AUGUSTA, GEORGIA 30901

Jacket design by Julee Bode.

Library of Congress Cataloging-in-Publication Data

Cooper, M.E. (Mary Ellen)
The greeter / by Mary Ellen Cooper.
        p. cm.
ISBN 1-891799-13-4 (trade paper : alk. paper)
I. Title.
PS3553.O59547G74 2005
813'.54--dc22

                                        2005004039

Printed in the United States of America
10 9 8 7 6 5 4 3 2 1

I dedicate this work to you, the reader,
and in loving memory of my mother —
the original greeter.
She always put a smile on my face, a song in my
heart and had a snack waiting on me
everyday after school.

ACKNOWLEDGEMENTS

To everyone, I would like to thank you from the bottom of my socks... because from the bottom of my heart is just not deep enough. Having said this, there are a few very special mentions that I would like to add.

To the reader, I am most thankful and appreciative. I'm glad you are here! Visit my Web site, www.thegreeterbook.com and enter your favorite greeter in our monthly greeter's award. Please send me an e-mail at drmecooper@drme-cooper.com. I would really love to hear from you!

I appreciate my family, Lee, Carter and Madison, for giving me reason to write and the time to do so.

Thank you Mom & Dad for all your acts of kindness! Dad, I am still looking for my beach ball!

I am grateful to Alice, who taught me not to question the ultimate plan, and to Marie for her intellectual support.

I give kudos to Alex, my buddy!

Special recognition goes to E. Randall Floyd for finding me! I sincerely appreciate this overwhelming opportunity.

I am especially grateful to the following:

Rev. Rich & Faye Bowen -- both have been guiding lights!

Rev. Bryan and Sharon Cockrell for show-ing me that even when life gives us questions that we cannot answer, we can still have faith. We will always remember the shining stars, Jenna and Daniel.

Kathy Layton and her family, we will never forget the talented Brandon.

Ripley MacIntyre, special gratitude in 104-degree weather to get just the right photo.

Special Friends: Carrie McCullough, Fran Tarkenton, Gail Hammill, Scott Yokum, Sgt. and Mrs. Jackson, Joey Brush, Lucille Gray, Mayor Bob Young and his First Lady Gwen Fulcher Young, Paula Deen, Sandy Roberts, The Kerlins, Vanessa Cromer, Crystal Wiggins and The Whittingtons to name a few.

Brenau University, Brenau Online College and Baker Online College for allowing me to teach outside box.

ALL of my students everywhere!

My current four legged, furry friends as well as those on Rainbow's Bridge.

Last, but certainly not least, the ordered path of God!

Oh yeah… about the gratefulness I expressed earlier from the bottom of my socks to everyone -- I did want you to know that these are clean socks -- honest!

I'd love to hear from you! See ya'll at The Store!

TWMA! ('Til We Meet Again!)

Mary Ellen Cooper

FOREWORD

In a lot of small towns, including where I was born – Albany, Georgia, – The Store has been a gathering place for decades. In the past, The Store might have been a local mercantile or hardware store, but nowadays, it's more than likely your local Wal-Mart. Let me tell ya, Saturday shopping is still alive and well in Savannah and all over. One day I was shopping out of town in Upstate New York and I was amazed how many people were doing their ritual weekly Saturday hunting and gathering. Now this was not some sleepy southern town, so that tells me this goes on all over.

I've spent many hours in Savannah Wal-Mart stores. We actually have four or five stores now – I've lost count. If you know my story, there were days I didn't have enough money for the parking meter in front of my own restaurant and I sure wasn't spending money in fine boutiques on clothes or anything else. I'm thrifty, since I was raised to appreciate the value of things, and I still refuse to spend tons of money on things I can easily get inexpensively in my own back yard. Now that I don't have to worry so much about money – I don't think I'll ever truly feel worry free – I still shop at Wal-Mart for everything from dish towels to chewing gum.

The Greeter is a story of small town life, small town values, suffering, joy and intrigue –

all revolving in and around the local Wal-Mart, its Greeter Miss Mary and Jazz, the teenager in charge of the shopping carts. He takes this job very seriously as does his friend and mentor Miss Mary. We could all use some dedicated employees like those two.

The Greeter is spiced up with my personal favorite topic – food – and Ms. Cooper's descriptions of our mouthwatering southern favorites like hoe cakes and collard greens are right on the mark.

I hope you enjoy Mary Ellen Cooper's warm-hearted tale of Jazz, Miss Mary and life in a small Georgia town.

Paula Deen

Author, Television Host, Entrepreneur

CHAPTER ONE

THE CLANGING OF SHOPPING CARTS hitting together in the cart corral could be heard at least a half mile away. It was a warm Saturday morning in April. He really didn't mind gathering up the carts from the parking lot — especially on such a gorgeous spring day.

Everybody had to start somewhere and this was his somewhere. He thought about why there were so many carts for such a small community. More than that, he contemplated how all those carts got into the parking lot and where all the shoppers came from.

Why did they call the place where the carts are to be returned to a cart corral? To him, it sounded like an old Western.

He had an inquisitive mind full of wonderings, but few answers. It was a new day, a fresh start, a beautiful Saturday morning in the small, rural southern town of Evanston, Georgia.

As it did all over the country, The Store breathed new life and hope into this little community. Wal-Mart was the life's blood of Cumberland Woods.

His thoughts were interrupted by the roar of a car engine passing by.

"Hey Jazz," Mr. Johnston yelled as he drove by in his silver Ford Excursion.

Mr. Johnston was the manager on duty. The Store must pay him pretty good to be driving that vehicle. Everyone seemed to like him all right, at least to his face. He was highly efficient and very organized. He went by the book on everything. Jazz guessed that made it okay.

The best part about Mr. Johnston was you knew where you stood. For him, a rule was a rule never to be broken or bent — no matter what the circumstance. Everyone got treated with respect, and all the workers at the Evanston store were considered the same.

Mr. Johnston sat in his car adjusting his rear view mirror then he checked his thinning, black hair -- followed by combing his mustache. He had entered the time in his life when he looked in the mirror and didn't always know who was looking back – he was in his early 40s. His hair showed a few grays.

Slowly getting out of his beautiful sports utility vehicle, Mr. Johnston waved at Jazz. Everybody waved at everybody else in the South – whether you knew them or not. He had been told by his daddy that this was a southern thing. He pondered why folks in other places didn't wave.

Jazz was a struggling, seventeen-year-old, young man who worked at The Store. He lived in this sleepy, little southern town outside of Augusta, Georgia, in a community known as Cumberland Woods or — as the locals called it — The Woods. The town had a caution light and one local restaurant — Home Café. Everybody knew everybody.

Ever heard of the Augusta National Golf Course? They play a little golf down there. Although Jazz and nobody he knew had ever been inside the Augusta National Golf Course, he heard the grounds were just magnificent.

Jazz was too busy in his own world to think much about the National, or golf in general for that matter. He had his own problems.

Jazz was tall – about six feet two inches – and thin – about 160 pounds – with a farmer's tan, because he spent a good deal of time outside gathering up shopping carts. His brown hair was streaked with natural blonde highlights most girls would pay good money to have.

He didn't figure himself good looking, mainly due to the few spots of acne on his face. He seemed to notice the flaws on his face more than others did. The blemishes seemed to be fading at a snail's pace as Jazz knocked on the door of adulthood. Before his complexion had a chance to catch up, circumstances in life had forced him to grow-up and take on adult responsibilities.

Jazz had a slow gait, to match his laid-back personality. He looked like a character right off the pages of a Mark Twain novel, a Huck Finn kind of guy. Still he had movie-star quality looks, but he didn't know it.

Most of the time, when he wasn't working, wearing his Wal-Mart bright orange safety vest, he wore a pair of dark blue jean coveralls and work boots he calls clodhoppers.

Jazz was about as southern as they came. His daddy had been known to laugh and say, "Well, boy, you so southern, if they ever cut you open, you gonna bleed collard greens and pan-fried cornbread." Then, his dad would let out a hearty laugh.

Collard greens are big, leafy vegetables. When someone is ready to cook the greens, the first step is to wash and look at each leaf to check for bugs and/or fungus. Once the leaves are torn off, they're put in a pot with some water and let cook on the stove.

When they're done, some hot pepper sauce is added — just to bring out the flavor of the greens. Pan-fried cornbread, or some folks call it hoecakes, are collard greens' sidekick. Any juice left in the bowl after the greens are eaten — the potlicker — is sopped up by the cornbread. Yummy, delicious, southern home-cooking!

Jazz could recall many a day coming home

and seeing his mother standing at the kitchen sink with her glasses on singing an old hymn like "I'll Fly Away!" and looking collard greens. She didn't talk much, but she loved to cook and sing. Sarah did both very well. Those home cooked meals from his mother were all gone.

Jazz had a great memory, and thoughts of the past often intermingled with those of the present. As far as his future was concerned, well… he was supposed to graduate from high school this spring. At least he hoped he would. There was still that incident to be cleared up.

"Good Morning, Jazz. How's that English class coming along?" inquired Miss Vera, a short, slightly overweight, forty-something-year-old woman who worked in the bakery department. Jazz's mother, Sarah, always told him never to trust a skinny cook – so he respected that Miss Vera was a little on the plump side. He had her a long time – she had worked in the elementary school lunchroom until The Store came to town.

Miss Vera was always nice to Jazz, so when she asked him to stay late sometimes and help her clean up or straighten up, he didn't mind. Jazz had a good heart, even though most people didn't know he was there. Sometimes he felt invisible.

"Fair to midland, Miss Vera. Thanks for asking," Jazz replied shyly.

Fair to middling was a term used to describe the weather, but some old time, deep southerners still used it to refer to how they felt when they're doing fine. However, it came out "fair to midland."

Miss Vera liked to read and often wrote a poem or two for a special occasion. At Jazz's mother's funeral, Miss Vera recited an elegy she wrote.

She usually asked Jazz specifically about English class, so he figured she wanted to know about his latest school paper. He was still waiting on it to be graded and returned. It was entitled "Why I Like to Work at Wal-Mart." Jazz thought he would at least get a C since Mr. Johnston's wife, Mrs. Clara Johnston, was his teacher.

He might not be too much on book learning, but in common sense he faired pretty good. He knew who to be nice to in town, but then again it seemed like most folks were pleasant to each other in general.

It's not that Jazz was slow — he just questioned everything. For instance, why did so many vehicles Ford put out start with the letter E? His folks told him as a child that he was analytical and took after his grandfather on his mother's side.

"Have you seen Mr. Johnston this morning? I really need to talk to him." Miss Vera said as her voice suddenly turned slightly anxious.

She was a real lady. Some said Mr. Johnston really liked Miss Vera a long time ago when they were in high school together. There were a few rumors here and there that Mr. Johnston and Miss Vera might still like one another, but you couldn't prove it by Jazz.

Everyone at The Store called the manager Mr. Johnston. Southerners called each other mister or miss out of respect, even if the person was only a year older. Youngsters called their elders by a courtesy title or their parents just might take them out back behind the wood shed for a serious discussion between their behinds and a switch.

"Yes Ma'am. Mr. Johnston is here. There's his S...U...V... over there." Jazz pointed to the shiny new Ford and said the letters very slowly with emphasis.

Jazz often noticed things others had, especially because he did not. He heard SUV meant sports utility vehicle, but he liked to say SUV.

The sun sparkled on Mr. Johnston's SUV like a brand new penny. Jazz took pride in showing off the silver vehicle, as if it partially belonged to him. He took pleasure in thinking perhaps someday he too might own a car he could be proud of – even if it did start with an E. Hopes and dreams were all Jazz really had.

"Miss Vera, I was wondering..." Jazz's voice trailed off. Miss Vera was already briskly walking away. Jazz wanted to ask Miss Vera about a rumor he heard the snack bar had been bought out and a McDonald's was moving in.

A store-bought hamburger every now and then with a milkshake to wash it down sounded really good to Jazz. Miss Vera usually knew the truth from rumor, so he wanted to check with her to see if it was real before he got his mouth all watered up. She would know something like that, especially if it had something to do with food.

Oh well, he had a lot to do and he really needed to get it done. Jazz's main job was to collect shopping carts from the parking lot and push all the carts back into The Store. Although most folks around there referred to carts as buggies, his official job title was cart pusher.

He was almost finished getting all the carts back into The Store through what Jazz called the short door. These doors were on the left side of the main entrance — a wide opening where Jazz could easily push the carts into The Store.

He worked the previous night – Friday evening. It was raining, as they say down South, like cats and dogs. Well, not really but let's just say it was a real trash mover of a storm. Georgia got a whole heap of rain in the spring.

Since it was raining so hard, Mr. Johnston told Jazz to go ahead and leave so he could spend some time with his girlfriend, Marsha Jean.

She was not really his girlfriend. Wow, he could only dream about that. Mr. Johnston was just teasing him, but Jazz really appreciated the thought.

Marsha Jean was the prettiest girl in the whole county, and she was smart, too. She had a 4.0 average in school, and she worked in the jewelry department. You had to be real smart, honest and responsible to work in that department.

Jazz came in early so he could move all the

shopping carts back in The Store before the crowd started coming in. Saturday was always a busy day.

His parents said Saturday was traditionally the day to get dressed up and go into town to do your shopping and bartering with other folks in the city. They both felt Wal-Mart brought back that old, familiar feeling of Saturday shopping. No matter what the reason, Jazz knew people were constantly coming and going, especially on Saturday.

Everyone in town and several counties around seemed to come in The Store, because they knew they could find whatever they needed. But this was not just any Wal-Mart; this was Jazz's Wal-Mart. Jazz noticed other folks also felt ownership about The Store. When folks traveled away from The Woods, they returned and talked about how glad they were to be back home at their Wal-Mart.

Suddenly, Jazz felt a light tap on his shoulder. He also smelled the most wonderful, light flowery fragrance. He hastily turned around, but he couldn't see who it was at first because the bright, morning sun shined into his light-blue eyes.

Slowly, he raised one of his young, thin hands over his eyes so he could see who was talking to him.

Then, he heard a soft, yet slow southern drawl call his Christian name. "Jes-abe, Cat's got ya tongue?"

Then, he heard a giggle. He was slightly shocked. Marsha Jean was standing in front of him, looking like an angel sent straight down from heaven. Every time he looked at her she had a special glow about her, but he never knew what to say to her.

The community referred to Marsha Jean as their local Brittany Spears -- but only in looks. She had long, naturally blonde hair, which the slight breeze was blowing, and the most beautiful blue eyes Jazz had ever seen.

They both had blue eyes, just different shades. Her figure was perfect – models would envy her slender form. She only wore a little make-up on her creamy, perfectly tanned skin, because she didn't need any more.

The management at The Store was very wise to put Marsha Jean in the jewelry department. Women liked her and men loved for their wives to look at jewelry, so they could look at Marsha Jean.

Often, women wondered why their boyfriends or husbands were looking at jewelry instead of visiting the other departments – like sporting goods or lawn and garden. One look at Marsha Jean and gents wanted to remain in eye-shot of her all day.

Everyone liked Marsha Jean, the all-around girl-next-door, cheerleader type. She would do you proud if you were with her anywhere. Any teenage boy would be proud to take her home to meet his mama. Marsha Jean and Jazz were seniors at Cumberland High School. They had known each other since they were babies. She always spoke to Jazz, but then again, she always spoke to everyone.

Jazz stumbled over his words, as if he had pebbles in his mouth. "Goo morning, Ma-ma-Marsha Jean!"

Jazz felt his heart fall past his stomach on down into his shoes. His face turned blood red from pure embarrassment. "I mean God morning …"

By now Marsha Jean, the Wal-Mart Jewelry Goddess – as she was called – was beginning to back up and walk away. "That's okay Jes-abe. I have to go. Mr. Johnston called me into work early today. Said he wanted to see me and Miss Vera about an urgent matter. Stop by my department today when you go on break… there's something real important I want to talk to you about, okay?"

Jazz couldn't answer. He felt like the dumbest person in the universe. He did manage to whisper "Good Morning" correctly as Marsha Jean sauntered into The Store. Jazz wondered what was so important that Mr. Johnston needed to talk with Miss Vera and Marsha Jean about. But more interesting still, Jazz wondered why Marsha Jean wanted to chew the fat with him.

CHAPTER TWO

TALL AND LANKY was the best description for Jazz. He was not athletic and muscular, like the football players. The whole town was devoted to two things — shopping at Wal-Mart and supporting the high school football team. The town loved their cougar mascot.

Jazz admired the football players and wished he was one, but his body was not built for fast activities. He often seemed to get the short end of the stick. But things started looking up for him when The Store entered his life.

Wal-Mart came to town about five years ago. Jazz knew a lot of folks were very glad, but some were real upset. At first he couldn't understand why they got their feathers ruffled. Now he was older and could see what was going on. Some in The Woods believed the little Ma and Pa stores would go out of business.

Some of those folks included Larry Thigpen, owner of Thigpen's Saw & Repair Shop.

Mr. Thigpen, and his dad before him, ran the family-owned business for almost 40 years. Jazz didn't understand why Mr. Thigpen got so upset — Wal-Mart didn't sharpen saws.

People still needed Mr. Thigpen's store to have saws sharpened. In fact, his business tripled because more folks bought saws and other tools at The Store. Mr. Thigpen was real happy Wal-Mart came to The Woods, after it tremendously increased his business. There were others who still complained about Wal-Mart, but Mr. Thigpen was the most vocal.

Mr. Thigpen frequently said, "Yeah ... I started a petition against it and now, looking back, I know I was wrong. I should have campaigned to get Wal-Mart into the community sooner!" Then, he would scratch his head and let out a chuckle.

JAZZ FINISHED his cart corralling for the moment. The number of folks going into The Store increased. He took a moment to be thankful for The Store and for the opportunities it brought to him. Here, he had the hope of making enough money someday to do some traveling. He was born and raised in Evanston and didn't travel – unless you count the few times he rode the school bus up to Atlanta.

At the end of the school year, the whole school got the county school buses together to caravan to Six Flags Over Georgia in "Hotlanta." Southerner's often call Atlanta "Hotlanta" — for more than one reason.

The only other times he left home were when Jazz's Aunt Inez and Uncle Carl from Jacksonville, Florida came up and took him as well as his sister, Sam, to stay a week or two with them during the summer.

Aunt Inez and Jazz's father were brother and sister. Jazz's mother, Sarah, allowed them to go to Florida as long as they promised not to let Uncle Carl drive. He had a problem with liquor.

Sam was Jazz's younger sister. Her real name was Sammy Jo Tyler, but everyone called her Sam. Jazz felt she was named right — she was a real tomboy. She could hunt, fish and climb trees as good as any boy in the county.

JAZZ LOOKED AT WAL-MART as a dream come true. He didn't realize when The Store was built it would become his future. It was Jazz's only hope. Growing up in such a small town, he had few opportunities to count on, and he was not planning on any higher education or trade. After all, his parents did not get much education so why should he?

His mother, Sarah Hardee Tyler, stopped going to school when she was in the fourth grade — there was no time for a formal education. Jazz's grandparents needed Sarah on the farm to help collect the eggs from the chickens. Sarah told Jazz growing up they had everything they needed from the land — she never went to bed hungry and she never took a liking to school anyway.

Nobody from the county went out to check on her when Sarah stopped going into town for a formal education. Guess everyone knew Jazz's mother was needed more on the farm than in school. Sarah struggled to help Jazz and Sam get a proper education, but she could not read very well, though not because of stupidity.

Years later, when Sam was about nine years old, she read about a learning disorder in school marked by some type of impairment that prevents people from recognizing and comprehending words when they see them on a page. Sometimes the person sees letters backwards, like a letter "b" looks like a letter "d."

Once she told her mother about dyslexia, Sarah sat down in one of the kitchen chairs in quiet devastation and began sobbing into her pinafore apron folded up in her hands.

"Thank you! Thank you, Sam! I thought all these years I was just plain stupid, that I couldn't learn like everyone else. You are my brilliant angel," Sarah exclaimed with pure joy.

Sarah asked her daughter if there were other people with the same problem. Sam embraced her mother and gently assured her there were. The next day at school, Sam spoke with her teacher who helped Sam gather some materials together to work with her mother.

Sarah and Sam had a grand time as Sam taught her mother how to read. It actually brought them closer together. Sam always wanted to be a teacher.

Jazz's daddy, Robert, helped too by asking everyone he knew to give him their old newspapers, magazines and books, rather than throw them all away. He told everyone it was for a school project the children were working on, so Sarah wouldn't be ashamed.

Jazz recalled it took his mother about nine months to really comprehend what she was reading. After that, she read all the time and even got a library card.

Sarah married Robert Homes Tyler knowing he did not have much schooling either, but he was a hardworking man who could see to the land. However, since Georgia Electric took Sarah's family farm, the Hardee Plantation, Robert had to take a job that required at least a high school diploma or a General Education Diploma –- what folks call a GED.

He studied for just two weeks before he took his exam. Well, low and behold – he passed it. Jazz always knew his dad was a quick learner. Robert explained to Jazz GED meant Good Enough to Dig another ditch. Then, he gave out a laugh, a sound Jazz loved to hear. His daddy's laugh was comforting. Everyone who heard it knew everything would be all right.

While Jazz was growing up, Robert worked various odd jobs. Sometimes he worked two and three at a time. Sarah took in ironing and cleaning houses for money.

When they lived on the farm, the Tylers were just barely making ends meet. Once they were forced to move to town, it was almost impossible. Even though their house was paid for, once Sarah got sick they had to take out a mortgage to pay for hospital bills and medicine.

Folks in town helped from time to time — the church and the community pitched in with food, clothes and, at times, money to pay the light bill.

Sam had brains and budding beauty. She was going places, though she might leave Cumberland Woods. Since Sam had such a high grade point average, she would indeed receive a scholarship for college.

Jazz was supposed to graduate in the spring, but Sam still had two more years of school. She might even graduate a year early, if she set her mind to it. Sarah made it very clear from the beginning that Sam was not to spend her time on anything but school — no chores nor job.

Everyone, including teachers, seemed interested in Sam succeeding. Jazz did not have the same support system.

Jazz knew he would probably spend his entire life in Cumberland Woods, working for Wal-Mart. He was very thankful for the opportunity. However, Jazz didn't know what would happen to Sam and him when his daddy passed away, except The Greeter promised she would be there. She was always concerned about Jazz.

JAZZ STOPPED THINKING about his family and returned his full attention to The Store. He thought about how grand it looked and how impressive the building appeared compared to the rest of town.

He took great pride in walking through the sliding glass doors, the grand entrance. Wal-Mart had the only automatic sliding doors in town. When he walked through those doors he felt he was somebody – a prince. He felt it was his store, his family, his future.

Above all, his entire outlook changed because of the job opportunities and the family Wal-Mart offered. Everyone in this small town and the surrounding counties knew where The Store was. The Store changed each of their lives in one way or another. Wal-Mart was the center of their universe.

Jazz felt a sense of pride knowing he was chosen to work at The Store — he was selected to wear the orange vest, which was for Jazz's safety. Before Wal-Mart, he didn't dare imagine working for a company that thought about employees' well-being. Jazz had only hoped he would find a job where he could juggle work and school.

At Wal-Mart, he only worked a few hours during the school week and more hours when there was no school, such as weekends or summer breaks. Wal-Mart had a rule for all employees in high school. Jazz felt blessed he worked for a company that cared about his education. When he finished high school he would apply for a full-time shift.

He dreamed of advancing through various jobs at The Store and ultimately wearing a red vest, one that indicated a higher position. He knew store managers often had college degrees, so he wasn't sure if he would reach this high and lofty state. However, he could dream — just like any other man. All the possibilities of working for years to come at Wal-Mart comforted Jazz to sleep on many nights.

EVERY ASPECT of Wal-Mart amazed Jazz. On this particular morning, as he walked through the only automatic sliding doors in town, he looked up at the tall ceilings in the front of The Store where shoppers grabbed their carts.

Jazz had never been in a building with ceilings so tall. After analyzing the unique architecture of the building, the first thing he noticed on this day was the sweet, fresh smell of cool air-conditioning — something most folks took for granted – but not Jazz. There just wasn't enough money at home to pay for air conditioning.

Equally astonishing for him was the number of carts needed for The Store to operate. Jazz knew if he didn't go out into the parking lot shoppers wouldn't have carts. He envisioned shoppers wandering around with items in their arms, trying to make it to the registers to buy everything – stumbling to their cars and then returning to The Store several times in order to purchase everything needed. Oh yes – Jazz understood the importance of his job.

He took in a deep, grateful breath as he turned to his left and saw a family buying some drinks out of the vending machines. Most folks put their change in the Wal-Mart brand drink machines and purchased the Sam's Choice colas. Why not? The drinks tasted the same and were a good deal cheaper.

Sometimes on Friday afternoons, Jazz treated himself and went to the break room where it was cool, while he enjoyed a Sam's Choice grape soda for a case quarter. Jazz daydreamed all week about how cool and delicious the drink would taste.

Jazz could get a drink more often, but he would feel guilty. His family was struggling and the thought of unnecessary spending when things were so difficult at home was not in his character.

Jazz didn't want to go to the break room and let everyone see he had no snack or drink. Most days he took his break in the snack bar area, pretending he already ate a snack in the parking lot.

Mr. Johnston seemed concerned about the employees because he made sure they got their break times. Jazz always believed it was real thoughtful of Mr. Johnston.

As far as Jazz knew, the soda machines at The Store were the only ones in town. He did recall a little gas station with a drink machine that vended glass bottles, right outside of town. The machine still worked — so the owner said — but he couldn't get anyone to refill it with glass bottles. Jazz felt dignity and pride knowing these were the only soda machines in town that functioned properly.

Next to the liquid oasis were two kiddie rides. Some folks walked over to The Store just to get something to quench their thirst, feel the cool or warm air — depending on the season — and let their children enjoy the rides in the front of The Store.

These drink machines and kiddie rides were up against a wall that divided this equipment from where the carts came in the short door. To the right of the majestic entrance were two games where customers tried to win watches, stuffed animals and various carnival-type items.

Looking at the games made him recall the previous month when he did not get a Sam's Choice grape soda for two weeks in a row. Jazz saved his two quarters so he could try his luck at winning a watch. He had never owned a watch, so he thought it would be nice to have one.

Unfortunately, Jazz did not win a watch, but he did win a stuffed white mouse laying his head on an emerald green four-leaf clover silk pillow. He thought it was really something.

Since Jazz had never won anything before, he was quite proud of his stuffed mouse. He won the mouse as he was leaving work for the night. But he was so proud, he went into The Store and showed it to everyone.

Workers as well as shoppers were glad for him, but The Greeter was especially thrilled. In fact, she offered to put it in a Wal-Mart bag — so nothing would happen to it on his walk home. Jazz saw the sense in this, so The Greeter shook open the blue plastic bag and he ever so gently laid in it his new prize he had won. All the way home, Jazz could not have been happier if he had won a watch.

He had many pleasant memories intertwined with The Store, and he desperately clung to them.

CHAPTER THREE

"GOOD MORNING, JAZZ!" The Greeter called out in her sweetest voice. She threw her arms out wide as if he was a young child coming home from his first day of school. Jazz fell into her loving hug as he relished seeing her and getting her attention.

The Greeter was Miss Mary Elizabeth Carter.

Everyone loved her — almost everyone. They called her Miss Mary, or Sister Carter, if she was greeting them at church. Little children who didn't have grandmothers called her MeMe. Around town, people looked up to her, and she was a powerful motivator — a rare person indeed.

If her name slipped a customer's mind when talking to someone, all the person said was, "You know, The Greeter, over at The Store." Then, everyone immediately knew. It was as if her whole existence was to be The Greeter at Wal-Mart — as if the job was created with Miss Mary in mind. This place, this town, these people in

Cumberland Woods depended on Miss Mary to keep their spirits high. And when things needed to get done, she made it happen.

Jazz, like all the others, didn't want the comforting hugs of Miss Mary to end. The hug was brief, lasting a few seconds, but Jazz felt the warmth in his heart all day long.

Miss Mary had been like a second mother to Jazz for many years. Since times first got tough, she often came to his family's house. They had had to move into a one-story, simple, wooden house when he was about four years old.

Hard times hit when they were forced to leave the family farm 13 years ago. He remembered his mother sobbed the day they left. His father literally picked her up and put her in the car.

Georgia Electric said it needed Jazz's family's farm for a power project, so the property was condemned. Since Georgia Electric was a public utility, it only had to pay fair market value because it had the right of eminent domain. Jazz didn't understand all those terms, but he fully understood the outcome.

Sarah said what Georgia Electric paid for the farm was not fair in anyone's market, yet it did pay for the house they moved to in town. After moving, Jazz cried himself to sleep on many occasions because he was so hungry — he prayed God would send some food.

Most of the time, soon after praying, Miss Mary appeared like an angel at their house knocking on the front door with a basket full of vittles. Sometimes the screen door was barely hanging on the hinges, but Miss Mary would try to dignify it by staying on the front porch until someone heard her sweet, melodic voice.

"Hey Jazz, Hey Sam, Hey Po' Boy!" Miss Mary said delightfully as if she had just walked into the White House and had seen the president. She was always glad to see everyone.

Po' Boy was a blue tick hound that showed up one day in Jazz's yard. The dog, later named by Sam, just stayed. The children played with and fed him what most folks would have thrown out. Jazz figured his family must have had some good leftovers because Po' Boy would hang around his house more than any other.

He always thought it was nice Miss Mary remembered the dog's name. But it was just like her to recall the little things most people forgot.

"Well, I cooked too much fried chicken," Miss Mary would say, holding her picnic basket full of food. "I made far too much potato salad. I rolled out and baked too many biscuits. To beat all, I can't possibly eat all of this hummingbird cake by myself. Do ya'll know anyone who's hungry and can help me out with this problem?" She ended her speech with a slight smile.

"I do! I do! I do!" Jazz and Sam yelled in unison with great pleasure. Even Po' Boy, who had been back in The Woods, came running and wagging his thin, frail little tail in delight.

In his mind, Jazz could still see that ol' blue tick hound licking his chops in anticipation of eating some good vittles. He was dead and gone now.

Through the years, there were many occasions where Jazz's family helped out Miss Mary when she cooked too much food. Southern cooking was one of Miss Mary's many specialties.

Miss Mary had a way about her where she didn't make people feel bad when she did something good for them. She made it appear it was not charity, but rather neighbors lending a hand to each other. In reality, Miss Mary was the one who always helped other folks out.

Jazz walked the back country dirt Georgia road mixed with red clay to Miss Mary's house many times — usually just to talk to her. The county talked about paving the road, but nothing happened. They often scraped it to cut down on the dust and mud.

Jazz figured the local government knew nobody with enough money lived down the road, so they didn't bother with the road too much. No matter. He knew he was always welcome at her house.

Sometimes, when he got there, he had to stand in line, but she sent a slight wave in his direction to let him know she was glad he was there and thanked him for coming to see her. Imagine that, Jazz would think in disbelief. Miss Mary thanking him for coming to see her.

"No, Miss Mary, I want to thank you for

letting me come to see you," Jazz always said.

"I am grateful to you for wanting to come to see me. Thank you," Miss Mary always said in return.

Then, they laughed and giggled like a mother and son sharing in a private joke only they understood.

HIS THOUGHTS were gently interrupted as he mentally came back to The Store.

"Oh Jazz, I am so glad to see you today. We have so much to talk about. Maybe we can get together during our breaks. How is your dad doing?" Miss Mary asked sincerely.

"Fine," Jazz said swiftly, as if things were better and he did not need to talk about it. He knew he would make a bee-line to the jewelry counter during his break to see what Marsha Jean wanted.

While Miss Mary returned to greeting customers, Jazz thought momentarily about his dad, sitting at home, dying with lung cancer. Some doctor said he only had about six or eight months to live.

Robert had been in the military and was stationed overseas for a while – where he started smoking cigarettes. He kept it up when he came home, but Sarah made him go outside to smoke.

Fortunately for the children, he quit before they were born. Some of his military friends said he got cancer because he was exposed to something called agent orange. Either way, Robert was very sick.

Sarah passed away about a year ago from colon cancer. At least that's what the doctors said. Jazz and Sam had grown to not trust doctors too much. His mother had been treated for nearly a year with antibiotics by doctors in Augusta before she was diagnosed with cancer.

The doctors said Sarah had some kind of stomach virus. The local town's doctor, William "Doc" H. Barfield, told her no one had a stomach virus for that long and she needed to go to a surgeon to cut her open to see what ailed her.

Sarah would not agree until it was too late. After a surgeon did operate, he told the family she might not leave the hospital because the cancer had spread all over her body.

Sarah and Robert had lived the way of hardworking decent folks. They were fine people with good morals and strong family ties, which included The Greeter.

Even though Jazz grew up knowing Miss Mary, he grew closer to her when Wal-Mart came to town. She had been there for Jazz and made his life more positive. She was always uplifting and had a kind word of encouragement for everyone. Miss Mary had recommended him for the cart pusher job at The Store. For this he would be eternally grateful.

Miss Mary didn't have much more worldly

goods than Jazz's family, but she kept her house clean. In the spring, she had red feeders all around her house — it was known as the hummingbird house. Her home was decorated with all kinds of pictures and statues of the tiny birds, even her mailbox was a giant hummingbird. She also wore a pin of one of the winged creatures on her blue Wal-Mart vest.

She drove an immaculate black 1969 Chevrolet Impala. Her mother gave it to her and she didn't drive it very often, but when she did she did so with pride. Jazz saw it on her face.

Miss Mary often declared, "It might not be much to look at, but my Mama gave it to me and it's paid for!"

Miss Mary walked to work on pretty days. She truly enjoyed walking and, for an older woman, she was in great health and looked well-preserved — though Jazz never thought how nice looking she was for her age until he heard other folks discussing the matter.

Jazz had seen pictures of Miss Mary when she was younger. She looked like a movie star. Sarah once told Jazz that Miss Mary had the classic look of the actress Helen Hayes combined with Mother Theresa's personality. Her long, mostly gray hair puffed out all around her head, though she tried to tame it by wrapping it into a bun in the back.

Though in her late 50s or early 60s, Miss Mary's creamy, smooth skin seemed to keep a tan all year that matched her charming hazel eyes. She always wore a dress or a skirt and top purchased from The Store. Her favorite footwear was a pair of slip-on tennis shoes made by No Boundaries, a popular brand sold by Wal-Mart.

Miss Mary wore a blue vest at work with "How Can I Help You?" printed on the back and several pins attached on the front. Some of the pins were awards from The Store for outstanding service — others she ordered from a catalog at Wal-Mart. Proceeds from the pins helped Wal-Mart's Missing Children's Network.

Pictures of missing children were displayed at the front of The Store on Wal-Mart's Missing Children's Board. Jazz had memorized the number: 1-800-THE-LOST.

People drove miles and miles to Wal-Mart, just to see The Greeter. They were all family to Miss Mary, though she didn't have any immediate blood relatives. Miss Mary was married once and had two daughters. Around town, people said she had twins in the late 1960s.

One twin was named Mary Elizabeth, after her, and the other girl was named Sarah Elizabeth, after Sarah from the Bible. No one remembered exactly what happened – except maybe Doc – but one twin died suddenly when she was about three years old.

All Jazz knew was people said Miss Mary blamed herself and so did her husband, Jack Lincoln Carter, though it was not her fault. After the little girl died, Miss Mary and her family moved away from The Woods. Several years later, Miss Mary moved back to Evanston — alone and a widow.

Most people in The Woods believed the surviving twin was raised with both parents constantly living in fear something might happen to her, too. Miss Mary never talked about her daughter who lived, but around Mother's Day yellow roses were delivered to The Store for her with a card that said "I still love you!" No name was listed.

Jazz thought that even in small towns, where everybody thinks they know everybody else's business, there were still things you only know when you live with someone.

The florist did not mind telling everyone the inscription on the card each year, but she didn't know who sent the flowers. Each year, the exact amount of money was placed in a sealed envelope and slid under the door at the floral shop with a typed message to send yellow roses to Miss Mary at The Store.

Jazz thought the flowers were from the surviving twin. He wondered where she lived and if she had a family of her own. He also spent some time dwelling on how everyone in town loved Miss Mary so much, but her own kin had nothing to do with her.

AS THE GREETER, Miss Mary let customers know where to go and sent them happily on their way. When necessary, she also told a person off without the person suspecting it.

Jazz guessed some of the employees were jealous of Miss Mary, because customers thought the world of her. She had certain characteristics that got on other employees nerves, especially their manager, Mr. Johnston.

The relationship between Miss Mary and Mr. Johnston was best described as cordial. There seemed to be a continuous struggle between the two of them. Jazz knew some about it, but not from her.

There was one thing everyone agreed on about Miss Mary – she never said anything negative about folks. The worse she said was, "When I see nothing, I say nothing."

There were times Miss Mary seemed to get away with things other workers could not. Jazz suspected Miss Mary knew something about Mr. Johnston that kept her job secure. Maybe it wasn't that at all. Maybe it was just because no one else in The Woods could be The Greeter.

All in all, Miss Mary was ideally suited to be The Greeter. Jazz often amused himself, thinking about various jobs and wondering exactly who would be suited for each job in Cumberland Woods. He could easily see the corporate office of Wal-Mart coming down, taking a picture of Miss Mary and declaring her The Ultimate Greeter.

Surely, every Wal-Mart wanted customers to be pleasantly welcomed when they arrived by someone who was genuinely happy to see them. One thing was for sure, Miss Mary loved being The Greeter.

MISS MARY WAS constantly involved in some type of charity work. This year, she was working to help Jazz's classmate Matthew Lumpkin receive a heart transplant. She started by asking customers for their spare change as they left The Store. She explained to each one the money would help Matthew's family to collect funds for the transplant.

Mr. Johnston found out and called Miss Mary into his office. When she returned to her post, she neither discussed the situation nor did she ask for money from customers.

About two weeks later, there was an employee meeting where Mr. Johnston announced Wal-Mart would help raise money for Matthew's organ transplant. Not only that, but whatever money the community was able to raise Wal-Mart was willing to match — dollar for dollar.

Miss Mary stood up, screamed "YES!" and started clapping her hands. Some of the other employees acted as if her behavior irritated them, and began looking at her like she was crazy. Then, Jazz stood up and began to clap, too. Eventually, everyone did so, but there was a look of reluctance on some of their faces.

At first, Mr. Johnston allowed Miss Mary to use a glass jar at her post. She would ask customers for donations as they left the store. However, she noticed that by the time customers got to her they had put up their wallets and purses.

Customers getting their change back out often created lines at the door. So, she asked Mr. Johnston if they could place a jar at each register. He agreed to implement her idea.

Jazz thought it was great to work with Miss Mary, and for a company that was always willing to help the community.

On more than one occasion, Jazz had personally witnessed Miss Mary's giving spirit. He loved her like a son loves his mother – after all, Miss Mary and Wal-Mart were about all he had left. She took care of Jazz and his sister, now that his daddy was too sick to work and his mother was gone.

When The Store opened up about five years ago, Miss Mary started taking Jazz and Sam shopping once a month. Though she didn't have much more than Jazz's family, Wal-Mart made it possible for her to give a little bit more to them than she could before. It stretched her dollar, she often chuckled.

Jazz was thrilled when they started these little shopping trips. Kids at school stopped making fun of his clothes when Jazz and Sam started wearing new Faded Glory brand clothes. They both felt like a million dollars, without the expensive price tags. To Jazz, the Faded Glory emblem meant he and his sister wore designer clothes.

Sarah was very grateful because the clothes wore well and looked great even after numerous washings over the years. After Sarah died, Jazz washed the laundry for the family, and he then understood the value of durability.

CUSTOMERS WERE bustling in and out of The Store this Saturday. Jazz stood at the front and helped Miss Mary wipe down carts that were wet from the hard rain from the night before.

Jazz's mind briefly drifted into a song and he heard the lyrics in his mind. "It was a rainy night in Georgia!"

Suddenly his thoughts were disturbed.

"Wait…Vera, what's wrong? Can I help you?!" Miss Mary called out quickly as Miss Vera ran out of The Store, sobbing.

"I can't talk right now," Miss Vera sputtered as she ran lickety-split through the door into the parking lot. Jazz walked to the door wondering if this had anything to do with the meeting Mr. Johnston called with Miss Vera and Marsha Jean. Jazz knew in his heart something was terribly wrong.

CHAPTER FOUR

"HEY, I SEE YOU BROUGHT your grandson in today. How are you doing, Harry the Fourth?" Miss Mary spoke directly to Harry, the three-year-old grandson of Harry Stillwell, III, and his wife, Laura.

Harry had fallen onto a car bumper a few weeks earlier. He cut his right eye and ripped the skin next to it requiring eight stitches. The doctor said there might be a scar and some damage to the eye. Little Harry the Fourth wore an eye patch and looked like a pirate in training.

"Granny said if I didn't cut up in The Store, I can ride the train when we leave," proclaimed Harry as if he were the heir to the throne, while he pointed at one of the rides. His speech reflected his age.

"We're going to toys right now to get a sword 'cuz I got my eye patch and I'm gonna be a real pirate," Harry continued without taking a breath.

Miss Mary turned to Harry's grandparents and almost whispered, "How is Harry's eye doing?"

Both grandparents smiled and nodded as if they didn't want to discuss it, so The Greeter moved the conversation along.

Miss Mary already knew from previous visits it was all right for Harry to have a sticker, but as part of her job, The Greeter needed permission before giving a child a sticker. The Store gave The Greeter yellow smiley face stickers for customers returning items as well as for the children.

"Can Harry have a sticker?" Miss Mary asked Mrs. Stillwell.

"Of course," replied Mrs. Stillwell.

"Yeah! I bet you can be real good. To help you out I am going to give you an exceptional sticker to help you be good in The Store," Miss Mary squealed with the enthusiasm of Harry.

As she pulled out a cart she told the pint-sized Harry, "This is going to be your special buggy."

His granddaddy lifted the tot into the cart.

"Now you must stay in the buggy with the strap snapped around you. I'm going to place this sticker on your shirt. You must sit up straight. Try not to wiggle around. If you keep this sticker on your shirt, when you return, if your Granny says you've been good, you can ride the train," Miss Mary told the boy in a serious tone.

"Yeah!" Harry the Fourth screamed with

delight. He sat up proudly in his cart as his granddaddy pushed it into The Store.

Customers near the door laughed while the little boy waved goodbye to Miss Mary. The shrill sound rang throughout The Store as Harry repeated the same question over and over, "Can we go to the toys now? Can we go to the toys now?"

Mrs. Stillwell stayed behind to have a quick chat with The Greeter.

"The doctor in town says he's unsure about whether or not Harry will see again in that injured eye, but old Doc said not to give up because the eye has an amazing ability to heal itself and do so very rapidly, too. We're keeping the faith he will see again. Right now we're trying to make the most of it by saying he is a pretend pirate. He seems to always be accidentally hurting himself," Mrs. Stillwell explained promptly.

She paused after she told all this to Miss Mary then she skedaddled into The Store. It was just like Mrs. Stillwell to say her piece and move on.

QUICKLY, Miss Mary turned her attention to the next customer. There was now a steady stream of customers coming in and leaving The Store. Jazz tried to help The Greeter by making sure she had enough shopping carts. He was always amazed she was able to do so many things at the same time.

She gave stickers to the children, placed

stickers on items being returned, pulled out the carts, gave directions to customers who were looking for certain items and stopped customers who were leaving to compare their receipts against what they were taking out.

The Greeter was the unsung hero of The Store. Indeed, she had so many things to do simultaneously and she never stopped smiling. She was the first person customers saw when they came in The Store and the last when they left.

Jazz figured each customer's shopping experience depended on The Greeter. Customers often came to her first with a complaint or a concern and she listened.

"WELL, SHUT MY MOUTH, if it isn't my boy Andy," Miss Mary beamed with glee.

"Hey, Miss Mary, it's good to see you," Andy Howard replied as he walked up to Miss Mary. They slapped each others hands as he went into The Store. The young man saw Miss Mary was swamped, and knew he would talk to her later.

Andy's father died when he was very young. When he was about five years old, his mother remarried and moved to Augusta with her new husband. Andy's stepfather was a heavy drinker and did not want him around, so he literally threw Andy out of the house when he was barely nine years old.

His mother cared more about keeping her

husband than finding her son. The young boy got involved with drugs while he was living on the streets and a dope dealer enticed him to deliver illegal narcotics. Andy's pay was a weekly supply for his own habit.

Miss Mary heard about Andy's situation and searched for him for six months, until she found him on the lower end of Broad Street in Augusta, under a bridge on a cold winter night.

She drove him to the Medical College of Georgia, several blocks away, where he stayed for many months in a children's rehabilitation program. During this time, Miss Mary gained legal guardianship of Andy. The parents would have been arrested, but they were never found.

He was smart and Miss Mary believed all he needed was a chance. The hospital administration recommended Andy be moved to a long-term care facility. Miss Mary agreed. The program eventually led him into a teen challenge program. Miss Mary stayed in constant contact with Andy and visited him often. During the summers and holidays, she brought him home to Evanston.

Andy was 28 years old and lived in Augusta where he was finishing his medical residency at The Medical College of Georgia — the same place that saved his life. He wanted to go into general medicine and practice in a small town. He drove out to Evanston, which was about an hour drive, but he didn't mind. Jazz knew it was to see Miss Mary, the only real mother he knew.

"HEY ROSE. Hey Rose. Hey Rose," Miss Mary repeated calmly.

There was no response. Rose Wilder just ignored her as she held her head up high and sauntered by The Greeter. Miss Mary was the only person who even attempted to talk to Rose. Everyone knew she as the town harlot. No one was real sure who the father of her daughter, Heather, was.

Rose bleached her long, curly hair blond, but dark roots constantly showed. She also wore a ton of make-up -- more than 10 ladies combined -- and cheap, gaudy jewelry. Neighbors always saw her in a tight-fitting outfit, though rarely the same one twice. If only Rose had a change of heart, a touch of kindness. Her jaded past had left her with a bitter attitude.

She had been married five times to three different men — the infamous Taylor brothers. There were a lot of people in town she needed to mend fences with, but especially the Taylor family. Word around town was none of the Taylor brothers spoke to each other because of Rose.

She was single now, but people said she was messing around again with the youngest Taylor, 13 years her junior. Some folks said Rose had contributed to many a falling out inside other people's homes as well. These disagreements might never be settled, because Rose was the kind to continuously meddle, so Jazz heard.

He noticed Rose never spoke to Miss Mary in The Store. Perhaps she was afraid Miss Mary might invite her to church. Another reason could be that Heather, Rose's only daughter, spent many a night on Miss Mary's couch trying to escape all the turmoil of the Taylor family. Unfortunately, now a Taylor grandson had his eye on Heather.

"Weeeeeelll, hello Mary! How ya feeling? You look as radiant as ever, huh?" inquired Dr. William H. Barfield. He was a fourth generation doctor to this community, but The Woods folks just called him Doc.

"Well, I'm doing better now that you're here. That radiance you are referring to is merely the reflection of you in my eyes," Miss Mary meekly replied. Doc and Miss Mary laughed and blushed at the same time.

A long time ago, Miss Mary might have married Doc, but for some reason, known only to them, she did not. Now and then they met at the Home Cafe for supper, and occasionally they drove to Augusta to catch a movie.

"Haven't seen you in coon's age Mary, guess you been doing all right? Doesn't look like any signs of you aging, huh?" Doc asked with a chuckle.

Doc was a gentle, mild-mannered man

who asked a lot of questions. Jazz guessed this was because he was a doctor and had to find out what ailed his patients. He was handsome for his age, well-groomed, white-haired and six-foot-two inches tall with broad shoulders and just a bit of a belly.

"I guess you want to be as healthy as I am, huh? You ought to start drinking a lot of water and walking in the mornings with me, huh?" Miss Mary mimicked his questions with more questions, trying not to chuckle too loud.

"Best be going to check to see if the pharmacist is carrying the medicines I will need to prescribe during the summer, huh?" Doc usually turned a statement into a question.

"Yes, you best be going on in, huh?" Miss Mary shot back.

They both laughed as Doc moved on toward the pharmacy area. He spent two minutes talking with the pharmacist and the next two hours looking at the various medications.

He still thought he lived in the time when doctors needed to have a close, professional relationship with the pharmacist, so plenty of medications would be on hand for patients when the doctor prescribed those drugs.

In the winter, the corner drug store carried various cold and flu remedies. Summertime required different supplies, like potions for poison ivy and bug bites.

The local pharmacy owner worried when

Wal-Mart moved in, but his store was still doing quite well. Folks came to town to go to The Store and while they were out and about, they took a stroll through the past at the drug store.

Customers still enjoyed hand-dipped ice cream and a walk through an old-fashioned relic. One by-gone artifact still hung on the front door — a sign to attract would-be customers in the past, "Free Ice Water!"

Doc knew about, but did not fully understand, the computerized system The Store had in place. With automatic inventory management programs in place, the computer would order certain medications to be shipped at the appropriate time of year. The Store had brought the computer-age to all of rural America.

Although Doc needed to cut back on his patient load, he didn't know how, even though he'd been feeling rather poorly. Like a lot of folks, Doc didn't visit a doctor when he needed one.

"Well hello, Carol, Dar-Dar and Manny. It's good to see ya'll today," exclaimed Miss Mary.

"MeMe! MeMe!" The children screamed with delight as they ran to hug The Greeter.

Their mother, Dr. Carol Sue Cummings, was a local celebrity – an online college professor from Augusta. Dr. Cummings could have lived anywhere she wanted to, but meticulously selected to come here to raise her children in what she referred to as "a place where time slows down long enough for me to watch my children safely grow."

Ever since she was on the front cover of the Evanston Times, people in Cumberland Woods recognized her. "Look. There's that woman Ph.D. who makes money teaching on the Internet. Imagine that," they whispered as Dr. Cummings walked in The Store.

Jazz liked talking with the professor. She was pleasant to him and even encouraged him to think about going to college – on the Internet. He didn't consider college an option, but Dr. Cummings might change his mind.

Imagine! There hadn't been any school opportunities for him, but The Store provided scholarship programs. And attending college online would mean he could stay in The Woods. But Jazz didn't have time to think about this. He was still wondering what Marsha Jean wanted.

"Thanks for remembering Matilda calls her brother Dar-Dar and Conner calls his sister Manny," Dr. Cummings said to Miss Mary. Both ladies laughed. Nothing went on in The Woods that missed the watchful eyes of Miss Mary.

Jazz decided long ago this was not because she was nosy, like some said. It was not because she had nothing to do; she had more than her fair share. Miss Mary truly loved and was worried about the folks in the community.

After placing three-year-old Conner and his two-year-old sister, Matilda, in a cart, Dr.

Cummings turned and proudly asked her son, "Conner, who was the first president of the United States?"

Conner confidently replied, "George Washington Road!"

Everyone laughed out loud, including Jazz. The main road running from Augusta to Evanston was Washington Road.

The laughter suddenly stopped when a man wearing a black suit and dark, sporty sunglasses briskly entered The Store.

CHAPTER FIVE

"WHERE IS MR. JOHNSTON? I need to speak with him right away," the mystery man demanded. Though Miss Mary was normally calm and able to handle every situation, this man slightly startled her.

"Turn to the right and keep going down until you see ..." Miss Mary began.

"I did not ask for directions to customer service, I asked to see Mr. Johnston. YOU take me to see him now," the man interrupted Miss Mary.

She saw the man was intent on speaking with Mr. Johnston immediately. However, she could lose her job if she left her post, even for a little bit. She regained her composure, straightened her vest and looked up into the stranger's mirrored shades.

"Follow me," Miss Mary directed the stranger, with a smile on her face, then to Jazz, "You be The Greeter for a moment."

Jazz didn't mind taking charge — he

dreamed of becoming The Greeter, the life's blood of The Store. The Greeter kept The Store flowing and working on a friendly basis. The first person a customer saw — the representative of the community — was none less than The Greeter.

Jazz figured if the first person customers saw at Wal-Mart was not glad to see the customers, then the customers' entire shopping experience would be ruined.

Some folks didn't understand just how vital it was to greet each customer with a smile as they entered and to wave to them on the way out, but Jazz knew. He watched Miss Mary do this every day she was there.

If he stopped to think about it, he would have considered Miss Mary might be in danger. However, he was too busy greeting people and helping them with shopping carts and providing information to worry about her.

As fast as Miss Mary walked, the stranger in the suit seemed to walk faster. At first, she was unsure of whether she should call security or find Mr. Johnston. As she approached his office she decided she would not leave until everything was all right. Jazz could see them from the entrance.

Not far from her post in the main aisle, Miss Mary discovered a spilled soda on the floor. It was a mess and she worried someone would trip and fall.

"I'm sorry, but I must call an associate to

come and clean this up before somebody falls," Miss Mary told the stranger.

"Okay, but hurry. I have to speak with Mr. Johnston as soon as possible," he demanded through gritted teeth.

Miss Mary immediately found a safety sign under a cash register nearby. As she placed the sign on the spill, Mr. Johnston happened to walk by.

"Mr. Johnston! Mr. Johnston!" Miss Mary yelled out, in hopes of catching his attention. She wasn't sure if he heard her, but his pace seemed to pick up as he faded into the men's clothing department.

The stranger realized Miss Mary was calling Mr. Johnston and started after him. Miss Mary decided to stay at the spill, until someone came and cleaned it up, though she felt oddly concerned about Mr. Johnston.

She called in a clean up request and some-one showed up to take care of the mess rather quickly. Miss Mary briskly walked through the men's department. However, Mr. Johnston and the stranger were nowhere in sight.

All she could do was return to her post. As she approached the front, the sight of Mr. Johnston relieved her.

"Mr. Johnston, is everything okay? I was looking ..."

"Follow me," he commanded. One thing everyone in The Store knew was Mr. Johnston didn't cause a scene in front of customers. He took employees to the side and had what he referred to as "a serious discussion." These deliberations were usually quite brief, to the point and he did most of the talking.

Mr. Johnston did not hesitate to bombard Miss Mary with questions. "Where have you been? Why was Jazz pretending to be The Greeter?"

She attempted to speak, but Mr. Johnston was in no mood for a conversation. He usually listened to what workers had to say, but not on this day – at least not with Miss Mary. Something was going on in The Store and Miss Mary, as well as anyone else, didn't understand.

"Whatever happened doesn't matter," Mr. Johnston retorted. "You need to go back to the front to be The Greeter. People are expecting to see you, not Jazz! Do you com-pre-hend?"

"Yes, I understand," Miss Mary responded in her most polite tone.

Mr. Johnston was walking away when Miss Mary finally got to ask him, "Did that stranger in the dark suit find you?"

"I don't know what you're talking about, just stay at your post," was the faint reply.

Miss Mary did not know what to do, she wanted her job, but she wanted to ensure Mr. Johnston was safe. Finally, she decided to simply do as she was told. Jazz heaved a sigh of relief to see The Greeter had returned.

"Really glad to see you back. There was a

couple that wanted to return a tie, a little boy in need of a fishing pole, a woman looking for you wanting your recipe for hummingbird cake. Then, there was a green Honda Accord that pulled up next to the door," Jazz rattled off then ceased for a moment to catch his breath.

"It's all right. You did a fine job. I'm back now. You don't have to give me a full report," Miss Mary replied with a smile.

Jazz was elated to be done. He knew her job was too much for him, as well as for most people. To be The Greeter required a special kind of person. He knew most people didn't understand all the Wal-Mart Greeter had to do. If they did, they would have appreciated The Greeter more.

Folks in Cumberland Woods and even back around Cumberland Lake didn't know what her job required, but they knew they loved her. They got special permission from Mr. Johnston each year and gave her a surprise birthday party in the snack bar area.

She loved it and so did the people in the community. Why, even Andy drove up from Augusta last year for the big celebration. Jazz figured there must have been at least 30 people there, a great turnout. He looked forward to the event coming around again.

Just then, the elderly Mr. and Mrs. Clayton walked in. Everyone treated them like royalty in The Woods because they were thought of in high regard. Jazz thought they had some connections to the Clayton Fruit Cake family from Clayton, Georgia, but Miss Mary said she didn't believe so. Another reason Jazz thought they were treated like royalty was because of their names.

"Hey Charles and Diana. How are ya'll doing today?" Miss Mary inquired.

Mr. Clayton spoke first. "Well, we couldn't be better. Could we Sweet Potato?" Turning to his elderly yet elegant wife he smiled.

Mrs. Clayton agreed with Mr. Clayton, "Well, no Sugar Pie."

The pet names were ironic, since both were diabetic.

"You both look like you have some great news to share," Miss Mary said insightfully.

Both Claytons began to speak at the same time, then immediately apologized. Afterward, there was a tete-a-tete on who would tell the story.

Meanwhile, Miss Mary waited on other customers. She learned a long time ago that Mr. and Mrs. Clayton were great folks, but they were so polite to each other it could make those around them have high blood sugar.

After about five minutes, Mr. Clayton continued, "Our son is coming to visit us," he said.

This was not just any casual conversation, this was an announcement.

"Yes indeed, our son is coming to visit us," Mrs. Clayton chimed in.

Then, they repeated themselves to Miss Mary in unison. "Our son is coming to visit us."

The Claytons had been sweethearts since grammar school, had shared a lifetime of love and just celebrated 53 years of marriage. Miss Mary had thrown them a surprise celebration shindig over in the church social hall last month with Jazz's help. Everyone who came had a great time.

"So you came to Wal-Mart to celebrate," Miss Mary interrupted. "That's wonderful. Is there something I can help you find? Do you need a buggy?"

"I have… well, after a lengthy discussion," Mrs. Clayton paused suddenly, regretting her words. "I truly hope I have not offended you by sharing with Miss Mary that we had a lengthy discussion," she said to her husband.

Miss Mary politely told Mr. and Mrs. Clayton to move over behind her so she could continue to pull out carts and not block the flow of traffic.

There was another exchange about moving behind Miss Mary, and how they did not mind doing so. Then, the conversation returned to Mrs. Clayton asking Mr. Clayton to forgive her if she had in anyway hurt his feelings.

"No, Sweet Potato, but I think Miss Mary is rather busy so we should briefly explain to her about our son," Mr. Clayton advised.

After knowing the Claytons for all of her life, Miss Mary knew they didn't have a biological son, yet she didn't know all of the details.

However, they loved telling the story of how they were blessed with a son.

Miss Mary thought fast. "I don't mean to be rude because I love to hear about your son Johnny, but you know, we go way, way back," she said with a chuckle.

Mr. and Mrs. Clayton did not laugh – instead they turned and looked at each other as if they needed each other's permission to laugh. Once they glanced into each other's eyes, a smile came across their faces. Almost in unison, they giggled. "You are so right, Miss Mary. We do go way back," they said.

Mr. and Mrs. Clayton were in their early 70s. Both had beautiful off-white hair like a fresh, hot bowl of grits. Mrs. Clayton's shimmering bob fell just under her ears. Mr. Clayton's was a wig though, because he lost all of his hair sometime ago. He used to tease people by saying he wore out his hair after years of thinking, least until Mrs. Clayton put an end to that silliness. His locks appeared so natural everyone had forgotten it was a wig.

They were about the same size too, around 150 pounds and five feet, six inches tall. Fairly lean was a good description for them. Jazz figured they didn't let eating cut into their shopping time.

They lived to go to Wal-Mart and joked The Store kept them alive.

Mr. Clayton did well over the years as a financial planner and in the insurance business.

Jazz knew he had a great deal of initials behind his name, CFP and CLU. Since the phone book was very important to Jazz, he often looked up names in the book.

Several years ago, when Mr. Clayton had a thriving insurance and financial planning business, Jazz discovered in the yellow pages that CFP stood for Certified Financial Planner and CLU stood for Certified Licensed Underwriter.

Jazz was not quite sure what it meant, but he knew Mr. Clayton was very smart to have so many initials. Most folks depended on Mr. Clayton for sound advice about their insurance, finances and retirement plans. He was in the insurance business for 50 years when he retired and stopped attending his various meetings. He said he wanted to spend more time in his vegetable garden and with his beloved Sweet Potato.

Jazz was thankful for the wise words Mr. Clayton provided his family to make sure they kept up the family's life insurance policies. Sarah's policy paid for her funeral.

Mr. Clayton was a member of the National Association of Insurance and Financial Planners who met the third Wednesday of each month in Augusta. He was also a faithful member of a Rotary Club in Augusta until he started a club in Evanston that met at the Home Café every Friday for lunch.

For many years, most of the business deals in town were conducted at the Clayton's home on Thursday evenings, beginning at 7 p.m. sharp.

Mrs. Clayton served little, heart-shaped sandwiches without the crust and extremely sweet, iced tea out in her formal dining room.

As the male guests of the community arrived, she greeted them and took their hats and coats. After she formally welcomed each of them, she politely excused herself to go next door to catch up on all of the latest local events, otherwise known as gossip, with the local ladies.

This was a weekly social occasion for decades in The Woods, until old age became a familiar face to Mr. Clayton and he retired from his associations.

Mrs. Clayton had a comfortable lifestyle. She had worked as a part-time secretary over the years at First Baptist Church on Main Street. She retired right before Wal-Mart opened. They lived well within their means. Jazz believed they could travel the world over and never put a dent into their bank account, but neither of them liked to go far from home.

Ever since The Store opened, Mr. and Mrs. Clayton came in The Store everyday. Most of the time, they took a stroll and looked around. Occasionally, it was to do a little shopping.

Jazz knew he could set his watch by them – if he had one. Every Tuesday they came to pick up their medications. But today was Saturday. Jazz's curiosity about their son's visit was building. Were they going to tell Miss Mary and Jazz the story?

CHAPTER SIX

JAZZ'S FIFTEEN-MINUTE BREAK time arrived and he could not wait to see Marsha Jean. A great deal had happened since he arrived at work.

He left Miss Mary with the Clayton mystery. It could wait at least until he returned. Knowing the Clayton's the way he did, they might still be there when he got back.

He laughed out loud as he passed the checkout lanes. One cashier turned and looked at him like he was crazy. The lanky, young man shrugged it off and kept on going. It did not matter – Marsha Jean wanted to talk to him.

The cart pusher decided to go to the bathroom first for a quick check in the mirror. He entered and immediately swirled around toward a mirror on the wall. He still had a few pimples on his face. Even though his voice was mainly set now, once in while he noticed it would squeak, especially when he talked to girls.

Jazz had never been on a date, and even if

he was interested in taking somebody out, there was no money. Miss Mary often helped him with money woes from time to time, but he could not ask her to pick up the tab for a date.

Wal-Mart helped him with school supplies. His job had greatly contributed to making the family's financial situation more positive. The money from the farm had paid for their house, but during his momma's illness his daddy had to take out a mortgage to pay bills and for medicine.

During these hard times, he was lucky to have a job and to be in a place where he could purchase food as well as clothes at a discount. He was grateful for his life; Jazz felt blessed. His needs were met. He thanked God.

Leaving the bathroom, Jazz caught one last glance of himself in the mirror and decided the boy he was looking at would not always appear like this. Miss Mary told him he was a fine looking young man who would someday be an even more handsome adult. He could hardly wait, but for now he looked for Marsha Jean.

Coming out of the bathroom, Jazz noticed The Store clock and realized he had wasted five minutes. Then, a cashier called him over – someone had dropped a bottle and water was all over the floor in front of her station.

Jazz trotted over to customer service and brought back the caution sign. The cashier was grateful and thanked him twice. He waved as he scampered away.

Quickly, Jazz went to see the Wal-Mart Jewelry Goddess. As he approached her department, he could see someone was crouched down behind the counter. He thought it was Marsha Jean, but he wasn't sure. Then, he saw a green vest.

Jazz leaned over the counter and said hello. Slowly, someone stood up. It was certainly not the love of his life. It was Mr. Roberto.

Mr. Roberto worked out in the lawn and garden department. Therefore, he wore a green vest. Jazz loved Mr. Roberto, most folks did.

"Hola, Mr. Roberto. Como estas?" said Jazz with a strong southern accent.

A few times, when Mr. Roberto had taken his family to the movies, he invited Jazz to come along. Mr. Roberto paid for his ticket and Jazz was always thankful for this. He respected and learned a great deal from Mr. Roberto. He even taught Jazz a little Espanola.

Mr. Roberto smiled at Jazz and spoke with a beautiful Spanish accent. "Muy bien. Y tu? I am sure you are looking for the Wal-Mart Jewelry Goddess, but she is not here. I have been here most of the day. She came to the jewelry counter about an hour ago so I went back to my department. Then a little while later, I had to go up to customer service and I saw Mr. Johnston and a man in a black suit come over to speak with Marsha Jean. Mr. Johnston asked her for her keys and to follow them to his office. She went with them, like it was no big deal. Mr. Johnston asked me to cover the jewelry counter again until their meeting was over. What's going on?"

"I don't know," Jazz said. He was glad to see Mr. Roberto, but now disappointment sunk in – Marsha Jean was nowhere to be found and his break only had about two minutes left.

Jazz thought the only good thing about not having a watch was it forced him to keep good time in his head. Mr. Johnston was a real stickler about taking your break and then getting back to work. Even though this was a part-time job, Jazz could not afford financially to lose it — his father and sister depended on him.

"Hasta Luego," Mr. Roberto said. "Catch you later, buddy. See you tonight at the spaghetti supper."

Jazz raised his hand in acknowledgement. Looking at the clock on the wall, he saw his break was officially over. He trotted back and found Miss Mary giving customers carts while checking packages leaving The Store. Simultaneously, she spoke to each customer.

"Okay... hello... happy shopping... okay... bye-bye now... hello... let me know if there is anything I can help you find... okay... bye-bye," Miss Mary repeated.

Jazz chuckled to himself. Miss Mary was still trying to tell Mr. and Mrs. Clayton goodbye. "Folks who don't know when to move on" described The Claytons. The Greeter did not seem to be frustrated or irritated by this though. Miss

Mary gave Jazz a slight smile and a hand wave as she continued to pull out a new cart for each new customer and to greet folks coming in as well as to tell customers leaving to "have a good day." She was like a friendly robot on auto pilot.

Jazz heard Miss Mary's tennis shoes squeak on the floor. Some rain from the night before had come off the carts and formed a puddle where she stood.

He jogged over to customer service and reported the potential hazard to Mrs. Sanders, who was pleasant as always. Jazz informed her about the wet, slippery floor in the greeting area.

Mrs. Sanders immediately found Jazz a mop and a bucket. She told him to keep it, since this could be a continuous problem.

Returning to the front, Jazz saw Marsha Jean leaving. He mopped in high gear. Then, he ran out into the parking lot where she was already in her little Volkswagen Beetle driving away. He managed to flag her down.

She slammed on brakes and began to back up. "Hey Jes-abe. What are you doing tonight?" Marsha Jean asked.

Jazz did not know what to say. His mind went totally blank.

Marsha Jean hastily helped him. "Yeah… I know how it is. Somebody asks you what you're doing and you don't even have your calendar or date book handy. Sorry to put you on the spot. Anyway, here's my card. My information's on it, my home number, address, and both my cell phone numbers. Just wanted to chat with you tonight about something that's going on you might be interested in being there with me."

Jazz stood in shock, but he did muster up enough courage to blurt out, "Are you in trouble?"

As soon as he shut his mouth, he knew it came out wrong. Marsha Jean had a puzzled look on her face.

"Well, what do you mean? I guess you're wondering why I'm leaving so early. Oh no big deal, but something is going on that has something to do with the jewelry and the bakery departments. I don't really know what, but someone has come in wearing a dark suit that is going to help Mr. Johnston get it straight. In the meantime, Miss Vera and I need to go home for a couple of days. The best part is with pay. Is that what you mean? Oh my, look at the time," Marsha Jean said.

Jazz wished he could look at the time, but he needed a watch to do that. Marsha looked down at her Peugeot watch her dad picked up for her in Paris last year.

Marsha Jean's parents, Charley and Marsha Faye Hollingsworth, were born with money. Now they were involved with a great company that sold legal policies to individuals as well as large corporations as an employee benefit. Everyone in town called Charley "Mr. Legal Lee."

The Hollingsworths seemed to have the golden touch in business, along with listening to

Mr. Clayton's financial investment advice. This proved to be a winning combination.

Mr. Clayton mentioned to The Greeter on many occasions how he admired Mr. Hollingsworth and if he were still selling insurance he would most certainly add Assurance Legal Plans to his services. He said it just made good, common sense.

Marsha Jean did not have to work and no one knew why she did – unless it was for the socialization and interaction. She said her parents wanted her to understand and appreciate good work ethics as well as working with people from various cultures and backgrounds. They knew Wal-Mart could do that for her.

Everyone in Evanston knew they could turn to Mr. Hollingsworth with any legal issue. Jazz understood Assurance Legal Plans to be like an HMO, except it was for legal issues.

His momma purchased a family plan, as Mr. Clayton instructed them. Both of Jazz's parents had their wills written up for the low monthly cost. Sarah wanted them to continue the policy after her death.

Another positive aspect Jazz noticed was that his parents talked with an attorney about everything. This didn't happen before Mr. Hollingsworth came to their house and signed them up for the program. Jazz made sure he paid that little bill first.

As Marsha Jean drove away in her new red

convertible Volkswagen Beetle, Jazz thought it made for a great scene in a movie or music video. Two teenagers in a Wal-Mart parking lot, the beautiful blonde girl drives away leaving the lanky, young boy standing there speechless.

Jazz didn't have cable television, but Miss Mary and Mr. Roberto did. Walking through electronics, he caught a glimpse of one or two videos. He saw some music videos at Mr. Roberto's house. Jazz's house just had books, the radio, audio tapes and great conversation.

Before his daddy got ill, Robert would make up all kinds of tales with Jazz and Sam as characters. They would also talk about school, life or whatever was on their minds. On weekends and during the summertime, they would often lose track of time and talk late into the night.

Jazz's mind jumped back to Marsha Jean as he began gathering carts again. His mind often wandered; he had a lot of time to think.

It was now mid-day and the April sun in Georgia was quite warm. As it beamed down hot and unforgiving, steam came up from the pavement. It was going to be a real scorcher; he could feel it coming. Jazz wanted to take off his safety vest, not because he was not proud to wear it, but because it was making him hotter.

Just then, Jazz jumped as a car alarm went off. He turned and immediately recognized the white mini-van with sliding doors on both sides – it belonged to Aunt Inez and Uncle Carl. He knew because of the pro-life bumper stickers.

Aunt Inez had accidentally hit the alarm button on her key fob as she tried to get the baby carrier out of the car. Jazz was always happy to see them, but about 15 minutes after their arrival he wanted them to disappear.

He thought it was because he was not used to being around children. There were five in this family, nine-year-old Robert, named after Jazz's daddy; five-year-old identical twin girls Bennett and Halley, named after comets; two-year-old Jasper, named because they liked the name; and two-week old Carly, named after the singer Carly Simon. Jazz did not know they were visiting from Florida this weekend.

The children all loved Jazz and jumped out of the car screaming his name. Customers looked at him which embarrassed him, but he still gave each child a big hug. Aunt Inez kept the sleeping baby in the carrier and immediately lifted the precious cargo into a shopping cart Jazz brought her.

"Well Jazz – you are a true sight to behold," Aunt Inez said. "Just a little outing for the children. I wanted to swing through Evanston to see ya'll. We're on our way to Hotlanta, but I don't believe it can get any hotter than where we are now."

They both laughed. "Going to stay with an old college friend over in Buckhead for a few days and take the children to see all the sites, like the Atlanta Zoo and, you know, the Cyclorama, a pictorial of the Civil War is right next door to the zoo, White Water Park and Six Flags if we have time. You know I like to pack everything in as much as possible," Aunt Inez rattled on.

She talked 90 miles a minute. This made Jazz nervous, like he was going to miss something. Robert said she didn't talk that fast until she went to Emory University in Atlanta. She wanted to be a gynecologist, until she met Carl. At that point, Inez dropped out of school and married him.

"It is fate Carl and I got hitched up together, we already had the same last name — Tyler — even though we weren't blood related. The best reason for me to marry Carl was so I didn't have to change the monogram on my towels," Aunt Inez said each time she told the tale. Then, she gave a slight sad smirk kind of laugh. Aunt Inez never said anything loving about Uncle Carl, yet she stayed with him.

Aunt Inez gathered up all of the children and told them to hold onto the cart while she picked up Jasper and placed him in the cart.

Even though Carly was just two weeks old, Jazz was amazed she and her mother were doing so well. He did not know anything about babies, but he was shocked they were even out of the hospital. Jazz figured he was like the character from Gone with the Wind — "I don't know nothing about birthing no babies!"

Maybe it was natural to go on a road trip when the baby was two weeks old. He really did not know, but he was very glad to hear they were just passing through.

Aunt Inez pushed the cart toward the entrance and Jazz walked beside them.

"Just saw Robert and he looks great, under the circumstances. Try to be optimistic. There's always hope," Aunt Inez merrily exclaimed. "Glad to see you, I am so proud of you and you're graduating, too. Robert is so excited. Well, we are going to get something to eat and stretch our legs. The kids and I, of course, wanted to see you, too. Maybe we will see you again when we leave."

She started into The Store, only to reel the children around back out the door.

"Jazz, don't bother your uncle Carl. He's in the car taking a quick nap, you know, he might drive later. Thanks, good to see you. Tell Bubba I'll call him when we get to Atlanta," she yelled.

He acknowledged by lifting his hand. She whirled the buggy around again and one of the twins fell off and bumped her head. Jazz could not tell the twins apart so he wasn't sure if it was Halley or Bennett.

Before he could walk over and help her up, she jumped back onto the cart. Jazz heard the baby crying. As they disappeared into The Store it seemed like all of the children chanted, "Can we look at the toys, momma please?"

Aunt Inez was like a whirlwind, but then again Jazz thought she had to be superwoman to keep up with five children.

Aunt Inez called Robert "Bubba" because when she was little she couldn't say his name or brother. She called him Bubba — for brother.

Since Aunt Inez's van was parked right next to the cart corral, Jazz went over and took a look at his uncle. Carl appeared as if he had been drinking and had passed out. No one could stay in a hot car with the windows rolled up and no air-conditioning this time of year in Georgia.

His dad told him all the drinking began after Inez married Carl.

Robert told Jazz that Carl was a descent enough fellow until he had a car accident that killed his mother. Carl was in a coma after the tragedy and therefore, unable to attend her funeral.

Even though the other driver was charged with the accident, Carl felt responsible for her death. His injuries left him in constant pain and he started drinking. He tended to talk too much and too loud when he was under the influence of alcohol.

On occasion Carl could also be mean when he was inebriated. Jazz briefly reminisced about the best trips to Florida — ones where Uncle Carl had drunk himself to sleep in the back seat. Once they got to Aunt Inez's house, Uncle Carl would go off with his friends — sometimes for days. Aunt Inez did not seem to mind.

JAZZ WAS GLAD it had been Aunt Inez's car alarm going off. He did not want to go into The Store and request an announcement about a car alarm going off.

Up until a few months ago, he would recognize who the car belonged to, go inside and find them. He then got the person's keys and silenced the alarm. However, Mr. Johnston had put a stop to that saying it was company policy to inform the shopper the alarm was on, the end.

He was right. There were so many alarms on cars, one could easily press the wrong button and then who knows what could happen. Jazz envisioned the police arriving in the parking lot while he would try to explain he was not stealing a car, merely trying to turn off the alarm.

Ironically, Jazz stopped daydreaming when he heard the sirens of a real police automobile and then an ambulance. Everyone in the parking lot froze. It was very unusual to hear both of these emergency vehicles tearing through Evanston.

Whatever was happening, Jazz knew it was coming in his direction. The police car came to an abrupt halt at the front door. Sheriff Rowe, a large athletic man with dark, wavy hair, jumped out and ran into The Store. The ambulance arrived next. As soon as it stopped, the Emergency Medical Team leaped out, got a stretcher from the back and disappeared into The Store.

Jazz began to run, hoping nothing was

wrong with Miss Mary. All the way in The Store, he had a horrible feeling. He began to pray.

"Oh Lord, please no! My momma's gone, daddy's almost gone, PLEASE don't take Miss Mary," he whispered under his breath.

As the sliding doors opened Jazz thought they had never opened so slowly before.

Miss Mary was not at the door. He did not see her anywhere. Jazz was speechless and his heart was gripped with fear as his palms became sweaty. Where was The Greeter?

CHAPTER SEVEN

FRANTICALLY, JAZZ RACED around The Store trying to find the police and the EMTs. There was a crowd in the pharmacy area. Maybe when Miss Mary went on break, she went to get her favorite vitamins and something awful happened to her. Jazz tried to peer through the crowd. He saw someone on the floor and another holding the person's head up.

"All right, everyone back now. There's nothing to see here. Everything's all right. Let's all go back to work or shopping, whatever you were doing. There's a sale on children's clothing today; check it out," Mr. Johnston said, scrambling for the right word to reassure the crowd that everything was fine. Nobody was listening.

No one moved. This was big time happenings in Evanston. Cumberland Woods had not seen an ambulance in a long time.

As the crowd parted a little, Jazz crouched down and got a glimpse of Miss Mary on the floor. NO, he thought, not Miss Mary, not Miss Mary. As he forged through the crowd with his heart severely pounding he saw it was Doc who was hurt. Miss Mary was holding his head and right hand.

"Hold on Doc," Miss Mary whispered. "You're going to be fine. The Lord's not ready for you yet. You still got children to help and old folks to see to. Come on now."

Jazz was crushed to see Doc turning blue — it looked like he wasn't breathing. Yet Miss Mary remained calm and talked ever so peaceful to him. Her tanned hand stroked Doc's beautiful, white hair. Jazz noticed the striking color contrast between Miss Mary's hand and Doc's hair.

Both had seen more than their share of trouble and their lives were intertwined with the people in this Store. These two people were woven into the community like the Manicar River that flowed through The Woods and into the Savannah River. Both were a source of unwritten and little-known history for these folks.

Doc's lifeless body was all crumpled between aisles 6a and 6b, right between the aspirins and the over-the-counter pain killers. Andy kneeled down next to Doc with his hands on his knees while he shook his head. It was hard for anyone to walk away from the horrible, yet loving scene.

Everyone was touched, in some way, by Doc. He had helped women give birth to babies for 40 years. After that he still did, if they could not make the trip to an Augusta hospital. He set broken bones as well as mended broken hearts — the town's doctor and counselor.

Doc helped everyone, whether they had insurance or not. Sometimes he traded his services for a good Sunday sit-down meal with all the trimmings. Other times, he bargained for a chicken or some household chores. Doc's prices were whatever people could afford. Jazz cut his grass and even washed his car in exchange for Doc helping out his mother.

Now, Doc laid motionless on the stretcher. Jazz's heart sank. It never occurred to him the town's healer could not heal himself.

Andy stood up and turned to help Miss Mary up from the floor.

"I did all I could do... all that I knew to do. I tried to give him mouth-to-mouth resuscitation, but it was too late, look's like he had a massive heart attack before he even hit the floor. I did all I could do. We were just standing here talking and..." Andy's words trailed off as he choked up and put his hand to his eyes.

Doc had been like a father to him, encouraging the young medical student with the sound words of an old country doctor. They had even discussed Andy taking over his practice some day.

Miss Mary hugged Andy and patted him on the back. "Good thing you were here too, so you did all you could do, son. Thank God you were here. The good book says 'It is appointed unto man once to die and then the judgment.' Doc had an appointment, just like we all do, son. All you can do is all you can do. You of all people got more knowledge about what to do than any of us. Good thing you were here," she gasped. Miss Mary choked back a few tears and began to walk behind the emergency medical technicians.

Everyone followed Doc's body as he was carried to the ambulance. There was no need to hurry, no cause now. As he passed through the great Store he loved one last time, one by one folks stopped to look at him as silent tears rolled down their faces. Jazz heard folks whispering about Doc.

"He delivered me and all three of my children."

"He found out that my grandmother had the whooping cough."

"Doc used to go fishing on Saturday afternoon with my dad and my uncle."

Dr. Cummings' son, Conner, didn't understand what happened. "What's wrong with Doc?"

His mommy did not answer, she could not answer. Doc was one of the reasons Dr. Cummings moved to The Woods — she knew he would take good care of her children.

Matilda answered as best she could from a two-year-old mind. "Doc's gone to sssh-leap! Right Mommy? Doc's gone to ssh-leap?"

Dr. Cummings just nodded her head in agreement. Doc had indeed gone to sleep.

CHAPTER EIGHT

LATER THAT NIGHT, folks gathered at The New Hope Church for the benefit supper.

"Are you okay?" The voice came from a faint distance coupled with the sounds of other people mumbling. "Sister Clayton, are you hurt?"

She heard people talking, but couldn't respond. The last thing Mrs. Clayton remembered was getting ready to go to church. Now, Miss Mary and Jazz were helping her up from the polished wooden floor in the church social hall. They plopped her in the closest gray folding chair.

Miss Mary made an announcement everyone in Hope County could have heard.

"Sister Clayton is fine," Miss Mary hollered. As Miss Mary coughed and cleared her throat, Jazz thought it was odd folks were called brother or sister as a courtesy title when they were at church functions.

"I do want everyone to be careful though, these beautiful floors are awfully slippery tonight.

Enjoy yourself and just go on back to what you were doing. The vittles will be ready in a few minutes. The Reverend Bentley will be saying a good, proper blessing then, so everyone just relax or go wash up, 'cause we are going to be breaking bread together in a minute for a good, worthy cause," Miss Mary reminded everyone.

The floors were not that slick, but Miss Mary did not want Mrs. Clayton to feel overly embarrassed. Miss Mary had a way about her that made everyone around her feel everything was all right, even when it wasn't. She was like a comfortable shoe. Even the first time folks met her they felt they had known her all of their lives.

The church spaghetti supper to help raise money for Matthew's transplant surgery was a fine example of her unselfish contributions. She had worked on this function for months.

"Sister Clayton, are you okay? You just gave us quite a scare when you tumbled," Miss Mary said. "Or is that the latest dance step?" Then, Miss Mary giggled.

Mrs. Clayton smiled. "I'm fine," she said defiantly. "Just can't see as well as I use to. Old age has a way of sneaking up on you until you finally resemble the picture on your driver's license. Know what I mean?" Both women nodded their heads in unfortunate agreement.

Jazz really liked the church social hall. He had fond memories of great times here with his family. He remembered ice cream parties after

Sunday evening services in the summer and chili suppers on cold winter nights. His mother loved to cook, so she volunteered to help out in the kitchen.

He counted the chairs and was amazed there were 100 chairs in this room. Folks sat down at their table with plenty of elbow room. Why, even the preacher could move his arms around when he was socializing and not hit anybody.

Jazz thought there was a real good turn out for the supper -- more than 50 people.

He had been told that whenever people gathered in the South, no matter what the occasion, there was going to be vittles! Food was a social event and had nothing to do with hungry people.

He thought it odd when someone had a baby or someone died, everyone immediately took food to the family's house. Jazz did not want to eat when his mother passed onto glory.

It was almost 7 p.m. and Miss Mary liked to start on time. Jazz noticed she was watching the time. Then, she glanced over to the Reverend Bentley and motioned for him to go ahead with the blessing.

The Reverend Bentley stood up and held his hands high in the air. Everyone noticed when he stood up because he was so tall. Jazz figured the pastor must have been at least six feet and four inches tall. He thought so because his father was about the same height and Jazz looked up to both of these men — in more ways than one.

With a booming voice, as if the clouds of heaven had parted and God the Almighty was delivering a command, the Reverend Bentley spoke. "Everyone bow your head and let us pray."

A moment of silence occurred while the minister waited for everyone to settle down and give God the respect he deserved. Folks felt the sweet power of the Holy Spirit every time the Reverend Bentley opened his mouth.

"Dear Heavenly Father, most worshipful God. Let us be truly thankful for the food we are about to receive. Let us share peace and kindness with one another as we break bread together tonight.

"Remember the reason that we are here to help aid Matthew on his road to recovery. We know that you have given doctors the ability to work and help us while we tarry on this earth to do your will. Therefore, Oh Lord, have mercy on us and Matthew.

"Also, Lord we want to remember Doc in our prayers. We thank you for allowing him to be with us all these years and we fully trust you know what is best for all us. Oh Lord, you said you would prepare our coming into this world and that you would prepare our going out.

"Now Lord, we commend all of these things into your hands and we ask for your blessings on this food as well as upon our lives that we have dedicated to your service. In the name of

Jesus Christ, Our Lord and Savior, AMEN."

"Amen," everyone said in unison. The crowd was not silent long.

"LET'S EAT! The line starts over here," Mr. Clayton broke the silence with delight. He was hungry and thought everyone's belly getting fed was delayed due to his wife's fall. Yet, Mr. Clayton would never say anything negative about her to anyone nor to her face.

Jazz never heard Mr. Clayton raise his voice to talk so loud, but he figured the old man's blood sugar was running low from lack of food.

"Would you like me to fix your plate, Sweet Potato? Or, would you like to go first?" Mr. Clayton said to Mrs. Clayton with a loving smile on his face. With diabetes, they knew how very important it was to eat on time.

"No Sugar Pie, you go first and I will get our drinks. Where would you like to sit?" Mrs. Clayton went on with their conversation.

Now, both of the Royal Couple were really delaying everyone from eating due to their overly polite mannerisms.

"ALL RIGHT you love birds, you honey-mooners. The rest of us are starving," someone finally declared from the back of the line.

A big uproar of laughter followed. Jazz believed the laughter was so loud and hearty the call to worship bell was slightly vibrating in The New Hope Church of God sanctuary next door.

In Cumberland Woods, there were two

churches, New Hope and First Baptist. The New Hope was a traditional, interdenominational, charismatic church. It didn't matter what members were or how they looked, everyone was welcome at New Hope.

There was a third church until about ten years ago — an African-American church way back in The Woods next to the Manicar River — Mount Calvary Baptist Church. Then, something mysterious happened. It burned down one Saturday in the middle of the night. The congregation arrived for service the next morning and was devastated there was no church! Some folks in the congregation had been going there for four generations.

The insurance company declared the fire was caused by natural causes, such as the strong lightening that night. Mr. Clayton went to the church site while the fire was still smoldering. He agreed with the Act of God report.

Most Woods citizens accepted Mr. Clayton's evaluation, because he was so well respected in the community. Only a few folks questioned the conclusion, but the Reverend Bentley said it would be best for everyone to believe it so no one would have to live in fear.

Immediately after this unfortunate event, the Reverend Bentley and several church elders, as well as members, went to the Mount Calvary Baptist Church grounds to meet with the pastor, the Reverend Leroy Jackson, and all of his deacons.

First thing they did was both ministers led their people in prayer. New Hope offered financial and physical support to rebuild the destroyed house of prayer. The Reverend Bentley also invited the congregation of the Mount Calvary Baptist Church to come and worship at New Hope Church of God while the building project was under way.

The Reverend Jackson accepted the offer of church worship and said he felt this was a sign to him the Lord wanted his flock to move in a new and different direction.

After much prayer and fasting for several months by everyone in both congregations, on Easter morning at sunrise the Reverend Bentley announced both houses of God were merging and would be attending New Hope.

The Reverend Jackson had read the church teachings. He found all to be sound Biblical doctrine and had no problem with the joining of the congregations. Also, the Reverend Bentley was pleased to say he would be the senior pastor and the Reverend Jackson would be the pastor at New Hope. Both men took turns delivering the word of God to all of his people.

The Reverend Jackson's wife, Mrs. Bessie Mae Jackson, offered to run the church kitchen for special events as well as Wednesday night suppers. Everyone was very pleased to hear this. You could not find a soul in town that was not familiar with the home cooking at Home Café owned by Evanston's one and only Mama Sugar.

CHAPTER NINE

AFTER THE CHURCH BUILDING and land was cleared where the Mount Calvary Baptist Church had stood, both congregations raised money to dedicate the land as a natural, bird sanctuary.

After the horrible burning incidence occurred, all different types of birds began flying into this area. The Woods people felt this was another sign from God — that this was a beautiful piece of land and he was pleased with his people coming together.

There was an enormous granite slab shipped all the way down from Elberton, Georgia, with the following uplifting inscription: "When One Door Closes, God Opens up Many Others For His Faithful Servants."

This was now where the entire New Hope congregation gathered for Easter Sunrise Service and Homecoming with dinner on the grounds in the fall. The grounds were just gorgeous with all kinds of flowers, roses and azaleas. The deed to the land was in the Reverend and Mrs. Jackson's names and they wanted The Woods to come to this place for quiet mediation with God.

When Jazz was about seven years old, the Reverend Bentley was assigned to be the church's minister and a great deal of wonderful things happened. The Reverend Bentley started a community project, Each One, Reach One! where each member of the church each week talked to, and even invited, someone to church with them.

Although Jazz had not yet brought anyone to church with him, he really believed this was a great program. The good pastor was always involving the New Hope congregation to do something good for the community and its people.

There was quite a stir when the Reverend Bentley first arrived in Evanston though. The very first thing he wanted to do was to change the name of the church. This really upset a great deal of folks, especially the older deacons. Some got mad and even left the church. Some started going to the First Baptist Church on Main Street in downtown Evanston.

Everyone knew the members of First Baptist were strict Baptist, and for the most part had old money, or at least more than the average Cumberland Woods citizen. For instance, that was the church the Hollingsworths attended.

Jazz often wondered why there were different churches. It puzzled him because he felt that no matter what, the basic church doctrine was the same. Although he was not involved in any deep theological questions like one might see on the Discovery Channel, he pondered long over some simple questions.

Jazz's religious thoughts were based on Christian concepts. For example, if Jesus was the only begotten son of God and whoever believed it would be saved and go to Heaven when they die, then why couldn't everyone worship together?

Jazz's God was simple — there was Heaven and Hell in the afterlife. Good folks like his mother were rewarded with a heavenly crown and bad folks well... he would let God be the judge. He had one fundamental religious thought — if you believed Jesus died for your sins on the cross and you accepted him into your life as your personal savior, then you prayed for forgiveness of your sins and Jesus would help you through this life as well as the next one.

His mother insisted he quote aloud John 3:16 each day. Jesus came to save us from our sins. He lived and died then was resurrected on the third day. Now, he sits in heaven on the right hand of God the Father.

This point for Jazz was really driven home when Mr. Roberto invited him to see Mel Gibson's movie *The Passion of Christ*. He did not cry during the movie, he choked back the tears. Later, that night and many other nights, Jazz cried in his room thinking about the torture Jesus went through just for him.

Jazz did not understand all of the fuss over religion. His God brought people together, not pulled them apart. His God did not care about how much money people had or did not have; he did not care about their skin color. Jazz's God loved them all.

Often times, in his mind, he saw his mother pushing him as a child in an old tire swing back behind their house singing: "Jesus loves me this I know! For the Bible tells me so!"

The Bible said it and that was enough for Jazz.

He did not care what the name of his church was. He knew his mother and family attended there and of course, Miss Mary went to New Hope. The church was always involved in doing something fun and different. It helped people in need as well... like Jazz.

Only bad thing was, the church was located way back in The Woods and made for a long walk. This was not too bad though. The walk gave Jazz time to think and mediate on the beautiful earth God had given him.

The New Hope Church of God looked like something right out of a picture post card. It was white, wooden framed with a tall steeple which enclosed a beautiful golden bell heard clean down to Augusta on a Sunday morning.

He did not know how many times he had walked up those front seven steps. Miss Mary had told him seven was God's perfect number. On the right side of the sanctuary was the church cemetery. Even though Jazz only knew a few people who were buried there, he often walked through and looked at some of the funny, old gravestones. Miss Mary knew a lot of people laid to rest there. By now, most of the congregation had their food and had sat down. Before Jazz fixed his plate, he went to check on Sister Bessie Mae Jackson. She kept a spotless kitchen and even though people were just starting to eat, when Jazz pushed open the swinging doors, he could see she was almost finished cleaning up. Jazz was amazed she could cook that much food and clean up so promptly.

Nobody made better spaghetti sauce and meatballs than Mrs. Bessie Mae Jackson — Mama Sugar. She pronounced it Shu-gah so, in turn, did everybody else. She also addressed anyone within hearing range as Shu-gah as well.

Jazz felt she really cared about him and he was just dying to know why the spaghetti sauce was so delicious so he came right out and asked her directly, "Mama Shu-gah? If you don't mind, what makes your spaghetti sauce so wonderful?"

She had just placed a blue, plaid fairly worn out oven mitt on her left hand to remove a hot lid. Mama Sugar leaned over a very large steel pot and dipped her wooden spoon in the red, thick, bubbling sauce. As steam poured out, she cautiously tasted the delicious tomato concoction.

Jazz saw Mama Sugar thought about what she should say. After a long pause, she put the lid back on the pot and rinsed off the spoon in the sink.

"They don't call me Mama Shu-gah for nothing… Shu-gah," she said with a broad grin.

Her skin was so dark that when she gave out a hearty laugh her pearly white teeth glistened. Jazz thought she would be an excellent model on a tooth paste commercial. Mama Sugar had the most beautiful, straight teeth Jazz had ever seen.

Mama Sugar was also very overweight. She wore a simple dress with her hair pulled back with an elegant comb to keep it in place. No one ever saw her when she was not wearing a long apron, the kind that went over her head around her neck and then tied in the back. However, she was so large the apron strings barely tied.

She cooked and ate a great deal. Her shoes reminded Jazz of nurses' shoes. She dressed for comfort. None of this mattered to the cart pusher.

She also believed in God's healing power and natural medicine from the herbs of the ground to cure what ailed folks.

"All right now, Shu-gah," she said to Jazz. "You have done an excellent job and now it's time to get your plate and sit for a spell. Let Mama Shu-gah finish cleaning up here." She patted Jazz on the back all the way out of the kitchen.

This was her nice way of telling him to leave because he was in the way. Jazz knew Mama Sugar well enough to know he needed to listen to her. She knew what was best. After all, she raised five children — all professional adults.

Of the five children, four were practicing medical doctors and the baby was in her last year of medical school at Emory University in Atlanta. Her children used natural medicine in their practice like their mother taught them. Mama Sugar said her medicine had been passed down to her from five generations.

Her four adult children doctors had a thriving practice down in Charleston, South Carolina, where Mrs. Jackson's folks were from. When the fifth child graduated this year, she was planning on joining her siblings.

Jazz loved to hear Mama Sugar talk about her kin in the Low Country. On the last Wednesday night of each month for the church supper, Mama Sugar always cooked what she called a Low Country Boil, which included shrimp, sausage, corn still on-the-cob and little new potatoes. This was one of Jazz's favorites and he learned from watching that the shrimp go in last.

Mama Sugar also cooked the best fresh-from-the-tree peach cobbler anyone had ever made. She said the secret was to let the peaches soak overnight in a little bit of lemon juice and a lot of sugar to bring out the natural flavor of the fruit. Everyone said the food was certainly better at the church since Mama Sugar had arrived.

The singing was better, too. Mama Sugar had a group of folks who sang the rafters off the church. They were known throughout the South as The Hallelujah Voices. She sang old-time gospel songs, mainly on Sunday evenings when the congregation was most laid back.

Jazz could see the power of the Holy Spirit shake Mama Sugar's body every time she sang. His personal favorite was "Oh Happy Day!"

He often heard the song playing in his head on the walk to church — "Oh Happy Day!"

The New Hope Church of God choir sang back-up and Mama Sugar took the lead vocal. When she started singing, she swayed back and forth while waving her white handkerchief that was anointed with olive oil from Jerusalem. Then, one by one, people in the congregation stood up and were moved by the Spirit. Some folks even raised a hand or both hands toward the heavens.

Jazz briefly remembered when Mama Sugar belted out a moving rendition of "I'll Fly Away" as they lowered the wooden casket that held his mama's frail, lifeless body into the ground under a huge water oak tree on the land her family loved for so many decades.

The song was still fresh in his mind a year later. Mama Sugar's voice was clean, sweet and melodious like an early morning songbird.

CHAPTER TEN

SUDDENLY, JAZZ REMEMBERED he was hungry so he picked up his plate and headed down the line.

On the other side of the serving table was none other than the prominent Mrs. Marlene Turnbow, a refined southern Lady in her mid-fifties. Jazz often pretended to be a movie star and he saw the world as it related to famous people. Mrs. Turnbow reminded him of Meryl Streep.

Mrs. Turnbow graciously motioned in his direction with her right hand at the deep, colorful Italian bowl. She always wore a big brim floppy hat and white gloves.

Jazz noticed the length of her gloves depended on the occasion. Short, wrist length for church gatherings and long ones buttoned up all the way inside the glove for more formal occasions.

Jazz heard she wore a hat and gloves because she had skin cancer many years ago on her face and the backs of her hands. After that, the doctor advised her to limit her exposure to the sun, and to always wear sunscreen on a daily basis and a hat when going outside.

Mrs. Turnbow had the most fashionable hats, Jazz thought, as far as hats go. He owned one: a baseball cap with Wal-Mart across the front.

Mrs. Turnbow was also a member of the Red Hat Society where, as she put it, "Disorganization is fashionable!" Everyone in Evanston knew when Mrs. Turnbow had a meeting because she came to town wearing a purple dress with a big red hat. She paraded around The Store before journeying to Augusta to gather with the other Red Hat ladies.

Very slowly, she spoke with a strong southern Georgia drawl, "Ja-azz, dear…could you p- lea-se hand Mrs. Turnbow the tongs so that I may ha-elp myself to some spaghetti noo-dles?"

Jazz smiled and nodded. He thought she was a real character. Everyone knew Mrs. Turnbow wanted to be addressed as Mrs. Turnbow, because she always referred to herself as Mrs. Turnbow. Also, she wanted everyone around to know and remember she was not an old spinster — she had indeed been married at one time.

She was wealthy, due to family money she had inherited from the cotton industry and growing peaches. Mrs. Turnbow often said she was the original southern peach.

Folks at New Hope used to wonder why she did not attend First Baptist Church — she had old money — really, really old money. No one gave this much thought anymore though. New Hope was just glad to have her as part of their congregation.

Her driver, a Black gentleman about the same age as Mrs. Turnbow whose name was Mr. Samuel D. Carlton, Jr., lived on her family's plantation in the main guest house which was about 2,300 square feet. Jazz noted Mr. Carlton and Mama Sugar made reference to themselves as being Black and not African-American, as he had heard on the History Channel.

Living in such a large house was a mansion by Evanston's standards, but a mere cottage compared to the 8,500 square-foot palace Mrs. Turnbow lived in, known in these parts as the Cotton Peach Plantation.

Hill was Mrs. Turnbow's maiden name. She was named Marlene after her great-grandmother on her mother's side who worked at one point as a nanny for President Buchanan's children — or so it was said.

The only manor larger was the Hollingsworth House at 12,500 square feet. This was the largest in the county as well as the four surrounding counties. Both mansions were built during the Pre-Civil War Era, but the owners kept adding on.

The same architect, Mr. David Aycock, was used for both estates' renovations as well as additions. The owners were quite impressed Mr.

Aycock maintained the original antebellum themes throughout the execution of the designs.

Although Jazz had never actually set foot inside either estate, he heard other folks bragging they had. Also, his mother read to him how large these plantations were from several articles in the Evanston Times.

There were rumors around town that Mrs. Turnbow and Mr. Carlton were having an affair, but this could not be proved by Jazz.

Years ago, Mr. Carlton attended Mount Calvary Baptist Church and Mrs. Turnbow went all the way to Augusta for worship. When Mount Calvary and New Hope merged, Mrs. Turnbow began to attend New Hope with Mr. Carlton. They didn't sit together in worship, but they traversed to and from church together.

After Mrs. Turnbow's father — a colonel in the military and a highly decorated war hero — died, Mr. Carlton became her chief financial advisor and he had done quite well in that position. Mr. Carlton frequently called on the aid and wisdom of Mr. Clayton for financial planning.

Mrs. Turnbow declared her approval of Mr. Carlton all through town.

"The Colonel, God rest his soul, after he passed over to the great be-yond, I was so blessed to have Mr. Carlton advise me on all of my financial matters. He has been a true friend to Mrs. Turnbow as well as the plantation," Mrs. Turnbow said, with one hand over her heart.

Mrs. Turnbow contributed heavily to the church, as well as community needs. Recently, she paid for the pews to be stained and the seats to be upholstered. Jazz was thankful for this blessing.

Some people said Mrs. Turnbow attended New Hope because a long time ago, she fell in love with a Pentecostal preacher, but her daddy did not approve. Instead, the Colonel picked out a husband from the well-bred, filthy rich South Carolina Turnbow family who made their money in shipping. They married, as her father highly suggested, then resided at her plantation as Mr. and Mrs. Edward Turnbow, III.

Unfortunately, shortly after the marriage the Colonel and Mrs. Turnbow discovered Mr. Ed Turnbow had squandered his family's inheritance. They were shocked to discover he was penniless!

At this point, Mr. Ed Turnbow was highly interested in seeing how fast he could spend Mrs. Marlene Turnbow's family money. He often stayed up late at night contemplating how to acquire other people's assets. The Colonel paid all of Mr. Turnbow's gambling debts and gave him $50,000.00 in cash to leave town with the understanding of never to return to Georgia. Everyone in town believed it was more than fair.

No one mentioned the word divorce around Mrs. Turnbow. She could be heard at just about any function when the subject was brought up referring to a divorce by spelling out the word in a whispering tone. "A d-i-v-o-r-c-e is a nasty end to something that once started out with a beautiful beginning," she would mournfully state.

This statement usually forced Mrs. Turnbow to choke back a few tears, followed by her excusing herself for a moment of solitude in the ladies' powder room.

Last anyone heard of Mr. Ed Turnbow, he was seen on various gambling boats traveling up and down the Mississippi as a waiter. Jazz thought Mrs. Turnbow had been through a lot and this was why she looked slightly worn out.

"Jazz dear, how is Wal-do getting along these days?" Mrs. Turnbow inquired.

"Fine Mrs. Turnbow, and thanks for asking," he stated with a slight grin on his face.

"You don't say! Well, I do declare Jazz. You would have thought that pitiful little creature would not have survived his terrible ordeal last year and be around to tell the tale or should I say tail… t-a-i-l. I made a fun-ny Jazz. You better laugh," she said as they let out a few chuckles.

Mrs. Turnbow was literally from high cotton, high society in the South so you would not normally see her carrying on with such foolishness.

Indeed, Jazz laughed. When talking with Mrs. Turnbow there were always three phrases bound to be heard — "You don't say!" "Well, I do declare!" and ultimately, you knew the conversation was over when she said, "I reckon it's time to move on. TWMA!" This was Mrs. Turnbow's way of saying she had other things to do and TWMA meant Til We Meet Again.

As they continued down the food line, Mrs. Turnbow said, "Wal-do and Mrs. Turnbow have a great deal in common. We are both survivors. He survived being hit by a misguided mode of transportation and Mrs. Turnbow survived cancer... now let me see here... going on seven years now, Jazz. That is why I am a proud supporter of The American Cancer Society and I always wear a pink looped ribbon on my blouse," Mrs. Turnbow said, as if she had beat the devil himself.

Mrs. Turnbow was, believe it or not, the local Humane Society all rolled into one woman. About a year ago, not long after Jazz's mother had passed on, he was leaving The Store and noticed a crowd gathered around someone or something in the parking lot. Jazz vividly recalled that fateful night.

He walked over and noticed a dog lying motionless on the pavement. Jazz saw it was a blue tick hound like his beloved Po' Boy. The dog had been hanging around The Store for a couple of days. Jazz wanted to take him home, but he knew he could barely afford food for the family — there certainly was no money for dog food. The stray dog reminded him so very much of Po' Boy, who had died about five years earlier from old age.

Jazz ran to the dog in the Wal-Mart parking lot to try to help him, but he was already limp, though he was still faintly breathing.

Fortunately, Mr. Carlton had driven Mrs. Turnbow to The Store that evening. Mr. Carlton saw the ruckus. He neatly folded up his Wall Street Journal, ever so exactly exited the Rolls Royce and approached Jazz.

Mr. Carlton could always be seen in a sharp, clean neatly pressed three-piece dark suit and a white starched-to-perfection button-down shirt. On hot days, he did not wear the jacket — only a tailored, long-sleeved shirt with a vest.

His pocket chain hung precisely four inches from the lower, right front pocket on the vest. Mr. Carlton made a point to tell everyone that after he dressed in the morning he measured to make sure his pocket watch was at this exact length.

Jazz thought it must keep the precise time, because Mr. Carlton seemed to glance at it constantly. He noticed Mr. Carlton took the pocket watch out of his pocket as if performing a military exercise. He affectionately referred to his shiny, gold timepiece as Little Ben. As he approached Jazz, Mr. Carlton had just checked the time and was placing Little Ben back into his pocket.

"My dear son, what seems to be the matter here?" Mr. Carlton asked ever so eloquently, each word sounding as if it were an example of the pronunciation from a Harvard dictionary.

With a solemn face, Mr. Carlton answered

his own question. "Never mind. I have accessed the situation and I am referring this unfortunate mishap to Mrs. Turnbow," he quickly said.

He then methodically pulled out his cell phone and pushed one button. Mrs. Turnbow must have answered immediately because by the time Mr. Carlton placed the phone next to his ear he said with much certainty, "Madame, I regret disturbing your pleasurable shopping experience at this time. However, there is a grave matter in the parking lot near the cart corral at the main entrance that requires your direct and immediate attention."

At this point, Mrs. Turnbow must have asked a question because Mr. Carlton replied, "Yes, Madame, the matter at hand does concern one of God's little four legged creatures indeed."

Then, as if making an announcement to the crowd, Mr. Carlton pointed at the dog. "I must bring the car over. Mrs. Turnbow will be transporting one of God's creatures to the animal hospital over in Augusta right away," he declared.

He turned and walked with precision to the Rolls Royce — a wedding present to Mrs. Turnbow from the Colonel, God rest his soul. Mr. Carlton drove back and got as close to where the dog was lying as possible. By this time, Mrs. Turnbow had arrived at the scene of the accident. Jazz was holding the dog's limp head in his hands.

"Well, I do declare! What has happened?" Before anyone could answer Mrs. Turnbow squatted down next to Jazz and the dog. Jazz was trying hard not to cry.

"Well, you don't say," Mrs. Turnbow remarked. Mr. Carlton retrieved a blue plastic tarp from the trunk of the car and a big, fluffy plaid dog pillow. He placed the dog pillow on the back seat and then walked over to wrap the dog up in the tarp so no blood would get on the car interior.

"Mr. Carlton, be careful now… you know your condition. I know how your back has been acting up lately. If you want me to, I will be more than glad to place the poor creature in the car," stated Mrs. Turnbow with real concern in her voice.

Jazz had the dog in his arms and was up on his feet carrying the animal to her car. Mr. Carlton laid the tarp down on top of the pillow and Jazz in turn laid the dog on top of the tarp. As he did, the dog slightly raised his head to gently lick the side of Jazz's face as if to tell him thank you and good-bye at the same time.

Mrs. Turnbow looked shocked. "Well, shut my mouth," she exclaimed. "Mr. Carlton did you see that? The poor creature just licked Jazz on the cheek. He must like you Jazz. I will let you know what happens to him. TWMA!"

With that, Mr. Carlton closed Mrs. Turnbow's door and the Rolls Royce transformed into an animal ambulance. Jazz waved good-bye as they drove away.

Several weeks later, when Jazz arrived home from school, his dad was swinging on the front porch with the dog at his feet wagging his tail. Jazz could not believe his eyes. Both his dad and the dog appeared to be as happy as two dead pigs in the sunshine.

His dad informed him that unfortunately he was only keeping the dog until Mrs. Turnbow could find him a suitable home. His dad had a slight grin on his face and then said: "Dog sho-nuff looks like Po' Boy, don't he Jazz? When I gets to feeling better, I'm going to take that dog hunting... that is if he's still here." Robert winked at his son.

Jazz wondered what he would do when she found him a good home. He felt happy and sad all at the same time. His dad slowly handed him a note which Jazz read aloud.

"Hi! My name is Wal-do because you found me at Wal-Mart. I understand that I am to stay here with you until Mrs. Turnbow finds me a new home. However, Mrs. Turnbow said that she isn't going to tell anyone that I am here and any-time I need food or shots to let her know, that Wal-Mart would always be willing to help out Wal-do!" It was signed with a paw-print.

Jazz was thrilled, but he wasn't sure who liked the dog more, he or his dad. Mrs. Turnbow brought by some dog food Wal-Mart donated to the local animal shelter and all of the dog's shots were up to date.

She told Robert the dog's annual shots could be received at Wal-Mart when they sponsored a day twice a year for pets to receive their shots for a very low cost. Mrs. Turnbow returned the dog in great health. Jazz thought about his brief, yet kind encounters with Mrs. Turnbow as they gathered food together that night at the church social.

"Ja-azz, look's like we have come to the end of the line so I reckon it's time to move on. TWMA!"

Jazz just grinned and nodded in agreement.

CHAPTER ELEVEN

ALTHOUGH JAZZ WAS HUNGRY, he had been concentrating so much on Mrs. Turnbow and thinking about how he acquired Wal-do he had put very little food on his plate. Still, he did not want to embarrass himself by going back, so he decided to find a place and sit down.

As he walked through the big social hall with his sparse plate, he could hear table after table mumbling about Doc.

"Isn't it a shame about Doc?" or "Did you hear what happened to old Doc Barfield?" These questions were followed by answers that sounded something like: "Well, I was in Wal-Mart today when suddenly …"

If Jazz had not been there himself he would have been more intent on listening to these conversations, but unfortunately he was there when it happened.

Jazz found the table where Miss Mary was sitting and, as always, it was full.

"Come on Jazz. Take a load off right here next to me, I saved you a seat." exclaimed Miss Mary with a big smile on her face. "I was just about to tell everyone a funny story about something that happened to me yesterday."

Jazz knew deep down Miss Mary was really heartbroken about Doc. She might as well try to do something good for Matthew, because she couldn't help Doc. This was so typical of her to want to go on and keep everyone's spirits up.

She was such a powerful, positive motivator. Jazz's dad said even Zig Ziglar could have learned a few tips on motivation from Miss Mary. Although Jazz's thoughts had drifted to Doc, he returned to what was going on at the supper table in time to laugh at the right moments.

"Sister Carter, you tell the funniest stories," Mrs. Clayton said. Her little tumble was a faded memory.

The funniest parts about Miss Mary's stories were they actually happened. She never told any that were derogatory to anyone. The stories were always light hearted and amusing.

"Sister Carter, you are a mess," Mr. Clayton chimed in.

Jazz's dad had told him this would have been a bad thing any place else, but in the South when someone said folks were a mess, they said "Thank you" because it was a compliment.

Miss Mary excused herself from the table to go around and talk to folks. Her personality was The Greeter no matter where she was. The conversation at the table quickly dwindled when she left.

"All right folks, I need you to listen up," Miss Mary said. She was going to make an announcement.

With a big Georgia smile on her face, she reached over to the nearest table and picked up a paper cup and a plastic fork. In one hand she held the cup and the other she held the fork. Then, she lightly tapped the plastic fork to the side of the paper cup. Everyone laughed. You never knew what Miss Mary would do next.

"We want to thank a few folks. I want everyone who worked in the kitchen tonight to stand up. Let's give 'em a hand," she said before clapping.

"I want to thank the deacons for allowing us to use the church social hall. I want to thank the Reverend Bentley's wife, Sister Carol Lynn, for the beautiful decorations on the tables. Isn't she talented? Personally, I can make silk flowers wither and die," Miss Mary said with a chuckle.

"I want to thank Wal-Mart for donating the cups, plates, napkins, ingredients for the tomato sauce and spaghetti noodles. See, there are extra benefits to working at The Store, other than knowing all of the town gossip!"

Folks shook their heads and laughed. "Now we all know how Sister Jackson does not like for us to carry on about her God-given talent of being the best cook in Hope County — or should I say the state. She won the Georgia State Bake-Off in the dessert category for her famous peach cobbler. Sister Jackson, come on out here and let's all give her a hand to let her know just how very much we love and appreciate her."

Everyone applauded, while only a hand waving a white handkerchief casually slipped out of the swinging kitchen door.

"Now, I want to give a special thanks to Jazz for coming early to put out the chairs and tables. He worked in the kitchen too. Also, I don't know if you know this or not, but he stays after you leave to help clean and put the chairs back up. Jazz stand up, and everyone clap your hands together to show him how very much we appreciate him," Miss Mary said.

The applause could have been heard all through The Woods. He felt like his mother could hear the recognition and she was proud. It was only a moment of clapping, but it could last a lifetime for Jazz.

He thought what he had done was nothing — anyone could have done it and no one would have noticed it. He could live the rest of his life knowing — at least for that night -- someone knew he was not invisible. Miss Mary wanted the community to know Jazz was alive and his life made a difference.

"All right now," Miss Mary continued. "We want to keep on helping with Matthew's transplant fund! As most of you already know the Lumpkin's do indeed have insurance, but it only pays 80 percent and since the transplant is suppose to cost around $100,000, they still need about $20,000 take or give another $10,000 for transportation and lodging depending on where the proper transplant is found.

"We have raised about $250 tonight so far — which is good — but as you can see we need a lot more. So, several folks have donated some sweets and goodies, like Sister Clayton has made some... ummmmm, good homemade sweet potato pie," Miss Mary said with excitement as she held up a small, paper plate with a slice of Mrs. Clayton's famous delicious dessert. "It's only $2.50 per slice — or a real bargain if you want the whole pie for just $10!"

"I'll take the whole pie," Mr. Thigpen shouted out. "Here's my sawbuck to prove it. Sister Carter you better stop trying to sell the best sweet potato pie this side of the Mississippi."

Miss Mary picked up a fork and started eating from the plate she used as an illustration. "Well... I guess I owe you $2.50 then 'cause this is MY portion," she said with a smile. She did a slight jig of a dance like a child who had tasted the batter from a bowl in the kitchen when the mother was not looking. Laughter filled the room.

"All right now," Miss Mary said at the end of her dance. "Is there anyone here interested in Mama Sugar's famous hot, fresh peach cobbler with real home-made churned vanilla bean ice cream?"

Mama Sugar still believed ice cream was best from a hand-turned old-fashioned churn.

"I honestly don't know how she finds the time to make real ice cream like our mothers did. Anyone interested in some hot peach cobbler topped with real vanilla ice cream?"

All the children in the room began running and scrambling while they yelled, "I am! I am! Me, too!"

Jokingly Miss Mary continued. "My famous hummingbird cake is up here and it usually goes for $10 a slice, but tonight and tonight only, for Matthew's transplant, I am going to let it go for only $5 a slice and the line forms right here. Come on now, this is for a good cause."

Folks were starting to talk by now, but those who heard Miss Mary thought it was funny.

People were headed for the dessert table and sure enough they paid $5 for a piece of Miss Mary's legendary sweet. She did make a great cake.

When Jazz was a young boy, he thought she actually put hummingbirds in the recipe! He chuckled to himself because he remembered how he wondered how many of those fowled friends she would have to catch to make such a large, six-layer cake.

If you gave her a half a second she would tell you the recipe she used was from one of Paula Deen's cookbooks. She knew it would always turn out perfect because she followed those instructions for a dessert that not only tasted scrumptious, but was pleasing to the eye as well. Miss Mary promised Jazz they would eat at Ms. Paula's restaurant, The Lady & Sons, in Savannah one day. Miss Mary continued to stand at the baked goods table until almost everything was gone. Then, she reached under a table and pulled out her guitar. She usually started out playing the six-string, after a few songs she would end up on the piano bench while she tickled the ivory keys.

As she began to sing some old hymns, one by one folks joined in. Different people followed Miss Mary by singing and playing their favorite songs by using her guitar or going over to the piano and plucking out a tune or two. Jazz could hear different conversations starting up.

Mr. Thigpen explained to a couple of children about sawbucks. "Originally back in the 1890s, the ten-dollar bill had an X on it. The X represented the Roman numeral ten; folks thought the X looked like the side of a sawhorse. Being in the saw business, my father and I still call the tenner a sawhorse."

The children said "Ahhh" and then ran to play around the tables without much appreciation for their brief history lesson. Jazz, however, found this to be quite interesting.

Jazz went outside to walk the Royal Couple to their car. They usually retired to bed about the same time the chickens did — early. He knew this would take a while because there was always a long discussion about whether or not Mr. Clayton would open his door first and then help Mrs. Clayton into the car or would he open her door first.

After a very long polite conversation, the decision was made to unlock and open Mrs. Clayton's door first, help her into the car and then walk around to the driver's side.

As Mr. Clayton was almost around the car, he stopped.

"Oops… almost forgot. Sweet Potato loves the smell of fresh air, hot or cold, winter or summer," Mr. Clayton said to Jazz.

Mr. Clayton turned around to roll the window down on her side of the car.

Jazz kept thinking how ridiculous this situation was. He believed people in their 70s should know by that age how they were going to get into their car.

As the couple slowly drove off, Jazz turned and looked up at the stars. It was a beautiful, warm spring night. He heard the old piano playing slightly off key while Miss Mary's beautiful voice sang out a familiar chorus. "At the cross, at the cross! Where I first saw the light and the burden on my heart rolled away," she sang.

He had a nice warm feeling inside as he was comforted by the thought of his mother being in heaven. Even though she was dead, at least she was no longer suffering.

The Reverend Bentley once told Jazz everyone had an appointment with death. His mother fought hard against her illness, but in the end the cancer won. He guessed it was her time, but he would have done anything to delay her appointment. Jazz figured death was the ultimate healer. He knew she was looking down and in some small way she was proud of him.

"Jazz, you are with really good people, in a peaceful place and I am proud of you," he thought she would have said.

Even though he was young, one thing Jazz knew was that happiness often did not last very long and was extremely fragile. So he had to hold onto these moments when they did occur. Jazz viewed happiness like ice being added to tea on a summer day.

CHAPTER TWELVE

EVERYONE WAS LEAVING NOW. A few folks stayed to help clean up; Jazz and Miss Mary were grateful for the extra hands.

The Reverend Bentley turned out the lights in the social hall, then closed and locked the old, squeaky, white wooden door. Jazz thought he would bring some WD-40 on Wednesday night and fix that annoying sound. He truly believed that between that miracle spray and duct tape, just about anything could be repaired.

Miss Mary offered to give Jazz a ride home and he gladly accepted. The ride was mostly a silent one. Jazz wanted to savor the happy feeling he had inside. As they got closer to his house he began to feel the reality of his problems returning. He could feel the ice in his hot tea melting.

"Jazz... How is your father doing?" Miss Mary spoke softly with a caring concern usually only heard from a mother's voice.

Jazz knew he could be honest with Miss

Mary. She was not like most folks who only asked to be kind. Sometimes people asked him about his father, but never stopped to listen to the answer.

"Not good. Dad was up most of last night coughing and not being able to speak. Sam and I take turns checking on him. Last night was my night to keep a listen out for him," he said.

There was no sign of the smile that had blessed his face earlier in the evening. All the funny laughter that had filled both of their souls just an hour before had faded quietly away like the dew on the grass when the morning sun rises and chases the moist droplets away.

"When we get to your house, I would just like to come in for a few minutes and visit with Robert if you don't mind. If it's not too late that is," Miss Mary said.

She expressed a true interest in his dad. Jazz did not mind Miss Mary visiting any time. He knew she fully understood what was happening, and she would give him guidance once everything was said and done.

It had been a long time since Jazz had heard his dad's real name, Robert, said. This day he heard it twice, the first time was earlier in the day from Aunt Inez. Before this day, he quickly thought the last time must have been when his mother was seriously ill and had fallen down at home.

"Jazz, I need you to get Robert," Sarah told

him that night — what seemed like a century ago. "I want him to carry me back to my bed." This was about two months before she passed and Robert was out back of the house cleaning his hunting gun.

"Miss Mary, you know you're always welcome in our home. I just need to go in and see if it's all right with Dad if you come in. I mean, more like if he feels like having company. Well ... You're not really company, but you know what I mean," Jazz said, his face burned from all his blushing.

"Son, I know exactly what you mean. I'll just pull up in the driveway and wait until you give me some kind of signal to whether or not I should come on in, okay?" Miss Mary ended her loving statement with a question not yet answered.

At this point, she pulled the car into the dirt driveway. Jazz got out of the car and took a deep breath. He began to get sweaty palms and his heart was filled with anxiety. Part of him wanted to run in the side door, while another part wanted to make a mad dash down the street and never look back. Once in awhile, the thought of going into Augusta and catching a bus to anywhere was a comforting thought for him.

Wal-do ran like a champion in a national dog trial to greet his owner. Jazz leaned over and petted the sweet-mannered dog as he escorted Jazz to the door. The dog gently nudged and licked the young man's hand. It soothed Jazz to know that whenever he returned home Wal-do was always there to give him a hero's welcome.

Wal-do showed him the side door as if Jazz had forgotten where he lived. His family's house was almost 1,000 square feet. Some folks called it a shot-gun house while others referred to it as a mill house. He called it home.

As Jazz carefully maneuvered through the dark house, he felt as if he were bumping into old memories. In the kitchen, he flashbacked to the many birthday cakes his mother concocted. He recalled the smile on her face as she opened the oven door year after year. For a moment he could smell the fresh baked dessert.

The cake had to cool before she could add real, home-made whipped cream and some type of fruit — fresh, juicy strawberries or blueberries she had grown. Sarah always believed fruit was better for her children than sugary icing. He smiled. She could make anything grow.

The front yard and the front porch were always filled with the most beautiful flowers. The garden out back grew the best fruits and vegetables. The house was clean and when there was enough money there was always a sit down dinner at 6 o'clock sharp.

Unfortunately, all of his mother's flowers and plants died with her.

He meandered into the dining and sitting area — all in one room. The lights from Miss Mary's car cast long shadows onto the wall. Jazz caught a glimpse of old photographs of his parents during happier occasions, like Thanksgiving when his aunt and uncle came up from up Jacksonville to celebrate. He grinned.

Next, he moved through the sitting area, remembering all the family and friends who sat around talking after Sarah's funeral about how they would miss her. Many of them made promises they would take her place and help the family out. Jazz had not heard from any of them since, nor did he really want to.

Only one had kept their promise: Miss Mary. He missed his mother and now he was standing over his father's bed wondering if he too would go to be with God.

Robert's bedroom was on the back of the house. The blinds were pulled up and the light from the full moon shown bright in the room. Robert, Jazz thought, was his name. Yes, indeed he did have a name.

All people said to Jazz and Sam now was: "How's your dad doing?" Their answer was then followed by: "What a shame!"

When Jazz was growing up and sometimes played baseball with the other neighborhood kids over near the Manicar River, his dad would come and watch. Folks would come by and call his dad's name. Jazz wondered why he was not called Bob, but he figured that if his dad wanted to be called Bob, then others would call him that.

A few called his dad Buddy, because he

would often say: "Hey Buddy!" whenever he saw someone, whether he knew them or not.

Robert was a hard-working decent man. He never hit Sarah, Sam nor Jazz. When he got upset, no one really knew it. He would go outside and take a walk down that dusty, dirt road. Robert was a big man with an even bigger heart, always helping others.

One time Robert had to go clean to Augusta for a part to fix the car, he picked up a total stranger on U.S. Interstate 20 who was coming from Atlanta heading over into South Carolina. The man came home with Robert and even spent the night. He had his car towed into Augusta the next day.

Every year, the business man traveled through Augusta and would always drive out to Evanston just to see Robert. Most of the time he wouldn't stay long, but sometimes he would eat supper and then keep on driving.

Oh, the stories Jazz could tell about his dad. One time, when Jazz was really little he got extremely sick with a bellyache in the middle of the night. This was the earliest memory Jazz had. He was scared too because there was a lot of thunder and lightening going on at the same time. His dad stayed up all night with him.

Even though that night was so very long ago, Jazz never forgot the refuge of his father's big, strong arms. The warmth and security of his childhood years were not filled with toys, but rather with love and happiness. Now, Jazz wished he could return to those days when he was being comforted instead of him having to be the comforter.

Just three weeks ago, Robert had to start on oxygen when he was sleeping. Each breath was becoming more and more difficult. Jazz blamed the tobacco industry for manufacturing such a brutal product that did not just kill a man but slowly drained all respect and dignity from his body until no one, not even himself could recognize who he was, even steal your name away.

The only way Jazz knew it was his dad was because he was there to watch the day by day sliding of his father into his grave. He watched as Robert was lightly sleeping knowing that his father was at peace when he was asleep for many reasons. Sarah was waiting on him along with Robert's parents.

Jazz was sure that his dad thought about talking to all those who had gone before him like relatives and folks in the Bible, such as Moses, Noah and Jonah. His dad especially wanted to talk to Jonah because Robert often said that he could truly relate to ol' Jonah.

"Yeah, my buddy Jonah. Got to talk to him when I gets to heaven. He and I see eye to eye, we like to run in the opposite direction when we see trouble in the brewing," Jazz heard his father say this in his mind. Then, he would laugh and grin bigger than any politician's smile anyone ever saw.

That was a long time ago — at least it seemed like a long time ago to Jazz as he stood in the moonlight at the end of a familiar bed that he had seen all of his life. He was now looking at a pale, thin man who had lost over a fourth of his body weight. He was frail, often needing help to the bathroom and back.

One thing Robert required was a daily bath and to put on his clothes like a respectful southern man would naturally do. For Robert, this was not a coat and tie but rather an under-shirt with a soft, plaid shirt on top accompanied by his work pants. The belt had to get tighter and tighter all the time just to keep them on his deteriorating body.

Often these days Robert would start the day by announcing to Jazz and Sam: "I don't cares how old and sick I gets, I want to be clean and have my clothes on to meet my day or my maker, which ever comes first." Then, Robert would give out a laugh that depended greatly on his energy level of the day.

His children did not share in his humor; they found nothing funny about his condition or this statement. Jazz did not mind dressing his father and working with him to make some of his last requests honored. He wondered if he should wake his dad or not.

Many times, Jazz and Sam discussed if anyone would come or even call to check on

Robert. Some called, but few came by to see them. Jazz thought everyone was just way too busy with their own lives. Actually, folks who did come by found it too upsetting to see him in such poor health, so they stopped visiting.

Jazz and Sam watched their mother wither, then die, with cancer. Now, they were forced to watch their father fade as well. Jazz had to wonder who would be next to get sick after Robert.

Jazz turned his thoughts to his dad. He smiled to think that this man he was looking at had a name and Miss Mary remembered it. A name gives a person dignity.

Robert laid there in his clothes. He had to wait until Jazz came home to undress him and put on his pajamas. Sometimes Jazz would not bother him to change because his dad told him only in his dreams was he no longer in pain. When was Robert's appointment with death?

CHAPTER THIRTEEN

IN THE DISTANCE, Jazz distinctly heard a dog howling. For a second, he thought about Po-Boy... sounded like Po-Boy, but he was dead.

His childhood dog had become his father's favorite hunting dog of all time. So many times his daddy would squeal with delight: "Son, that dog can hunt. Daddy means it. Got-a-mighty knows. That dog can hunt!" Robert was what they call down South a good 'ole boy. "Got-a-mighty knows!" Robert would declare.

"God almighty knows" means whatever you are saying is the gospel truth. His English was not always correct and his manners were not quite fit for a state dinner at the White House, but he was likeable. He helped out anyone in need.

Robert had been too sick to fully train Wal-do on hunting, yet Jazz knew the dog was a natural — all Wal-do needed was a buddy.

Visitors were few and far between, but Robert sure did enjoy the occasional drop in with

Miss Mary. The ladies seemed to pour into the house after his mother died until they discovered Robert was seriously ill. Robert only seemed to fancy Miss Mary.

Jazz often relished the thought that if his father had not gotten so sick, perhaps he and Miss Mary might have enjoyed a romantic relationship — even married. However, lung cancer was killing Robert as well as Jazz's dream of Miss Mary ever being a stepmother.

"Dad? Dad, Miss Mary's here and wants to come in for a little visit. Do you feel like some company?" Softly, but firmly, Jazz woke his father.

"What? Jazz is that you! Am I... uh... where am I?" Robert weakly answered with a trace of confusion in his voice. Jazz had been told chemotherapy would often make his dad confused. From what he had seen, he agreed.

"Dad, it's me, Jazz. Miss Mary just brought me home from the spaghetti supper over at the church. She wants to come in and chew the fat with you for a spell. Can you come in the sitting room?"

Jazz talked a little louder now. Robert did not say a word, only sat up in the bed and shook his head real hard as he pulled off the oxygen mask from his face. He refused the offer of assistance as he stood up and walked to the hall bathroom.

Jazz could see him combing his gorgeous

Robert Redford hair in the medicine cabinet mirror on the wall with two panels. His dad could have been the famous actor's body double before the illness struck.

From where Jazz was standing now, his dad appeared to have two faces. Then, Robert began to brush his teeth. With a mouth full of toothpaste and toothbrush, Robert proclaimed, "Well, don't jus stand da. Go geet her."

Jazz laughed. He'd been around his father long enough to know that it was time to move and go invite Miss Mary to come in. As he ran back through the house that was full of so many memories, he was pleased, because for a moment it felt like his strong, tall, handsome, energetic dad was back.

Jazz ran quickly out to the car. He was almost out of breath, he wanted Miss Mary to come in to see his real dad, his old dad, the man named Robert before the sick dying dad with a disease returned. Robert had made a quick transformation — if only temporarily. Jazz was elated.

"Come on in, Miss Mary. Dad really wants to see you," Jazz said, huffing and puffing from running combined with the excitement.

Miss Mary did not tell Jazz to catch his breath or to calm down. She was thrilled to see him so happy. "Okay, let's go!" she replied without hesitation.

Robert turned on the porch lights as well as in the house so Miss Mary and Jazz could see.

The sitting room was filled with old furniture.

The house smelled a slight bit musty from the dust. The children took turns cleaning the house on Fridays, but it was not the same since Sarah died, the house as well as the family.

The room was filled with pictures chronicling the children's school days — including a family portrait taken the year before Sarah passed away. They all looked so happy and content to be together. Jazz often wished things were like that picture — his mother alive and everyone happy.

Sitting in his favorite overstuffed, worn out faded green chair, Robert looked like King Robert. He rose to his feet with pride and a natural grin spread across his face as if he had just opened an envelope with an unexpected rebate check from the government.

Jazz knew that look because each month when his father got his government pension check for military service, Robert looked like that. The check was not much, but every bit helped, as Sarah would have said.

"Well, my oh, oh my, OH MY. Now, aren't you a sight for sore eyes, Mr. Tyler," Miss Mary said.

The laughter of Robert, Jazz and Miss Mary intertwined then ascended into the heavens as if sending up a signal to Sarah, "We're all here and everything is going to be just fine."

Yes, indeed Jazz was comforted with the thought that everything indeed was all right, at least for tonight.

"Mary, sit down here. Right next to me so I can see you and hold your lovely hand. We will give the neighbors something to talk about," Robert said.

They all laughed as Jazz lowered his head in embarrassment. Peacefulness filled the air as he quietly slipped into the kitchen to make some sunshine tea — half lemonade and half sweet tea. Sarah taught Jazz how to make this delicious beverage for special occasions. Indeed, this was a special occasion.

As he made the tea, he could hear his mother's voice faintly, "Southerners love their tea cold and sweet. We don't believe tea is sweet enough until the spoon can stand up straight in the glass all by itself."

Everyone in the family always laughed and agreed.

Jazz made four glasses of the sunshine tea, also known in some parts as Arnold Palmer tea. Without a word, he returned to the sitting room with two of the glasses.

There was a stack of stone coasters with hand-painted flowers on the marble-top side table next to his daddy's chair. He took great pride in those coasters — he bought them for his mother as a present the last Mother's Day she was alive. Jazz had bought the set from The Store and was able to use his 10 percent discount, and the items were on sale.

He wanted something special to come from him and Sam that year, something they could remember. He still recalled the look on his mother's face when she opened the present.

"Why Sam, Jazz? I do declare. This was the most wonderful present that any son and daughter could've given their mother. This will go perfectly on the marble top. Thank ya'll. I love you both so much," she cried as she hugged them at the same time.

Jazz secretly thanked God for Wal-Mart and his job there. Without The Store, Sarah's last Mother's Day would have had no present, no stone coasters. Even now, Jazz thought for a moment about his reason for getting the drinks. Was it because he wanted to be polite and offer his guest a refreshing beverage or did he want an opportunity to show off the beautiful coasters?

"Thanks, Jazz," Robert and Miss Mary acknowledged in unison.

Then, they both turned and gave each other a glance as if they were a school boy and girl waiting for the other one to start a conversation. The giggling continued as Jazz excused himself.

Neither Robert nor Miss Mary noticed Jazz exit the room. He had turned invisible again, but this time he did not mind so much. He was very glad to see his father so happy for a change, even if it was for just a little time.

Jazz returned to the kitchen and picked up

the other two glasses of sunshine tea. Walking back through the sitting room, Jazz could hear the two talking like old times. They were reminiscing about when life was not so complicated and there were fewer decisions to be made — when life was a choice rather than an endless road of uncontrollable events.

Softly with his foot, Jazz knocked on his sister's bedroom door. He knew she was still awake because her light was on.

"Just a minute," Sam mumbled in a tired voice.

As he waited, Jazz glanced down at his shoes. He could hear his mother's voice faintly in his mind, "Jesabe, what are you doing wearing shoes in this house?"

One thing about Jazz's mother was she kept a clean house. He silently pledged he would do better about not wearing shoes in the house.

The door opened and the most beautiful 15-year-old girl stood there. Jazz did not notice Sam was attractive. He knew boys at school had noticed but he did not. Sam looked like their mother and acted like their father. Perhaps this was why Sarah did not always understand Sam.

Jazz and his mother seemed to be more like two peas in a pod. The best description for Sammy Jo Tyler was she looked like she could have been the younger sister to movie star Daryl Hannah. At least, that was who Jazz heard the guys at school compare her to. He looked up to the movies, a fantasy world that was much different from his own.

Jazz handed Sam the glass of cool refreshment. She was grateful and immediately began gulping down the ice-cold sweet beverage.

"Thanks Jazz. What's the special occasion?" Sam had a puzzled look on her angelic face. She was working hard, but then again she was always diligent about her school assignments. Jazz was very proud of her and really wanted her to do well in school. Sam had a good chance at the world with a great education.

"Miss Mary just brought me home from the church spaghetti supper. Oops… that reminds me, do you want some spaghetti? There were some leftovers and I said I would take them. I left them out in her car but I can run out and get them. Be glad to warm it up for you." Jazz was glad he offered to get her some spaghetti — he would have hated to leave it in Miss Mary's car.

"No thanks, but that's funny. I fixed Dad and me some spaghetti tonight as well." They both enjoyed a good chuckle.

"I was just studying for finals," Sam said. "You know, you better hit the books yourself. Have you heard anything about graduation yet? Have you had a chance to…"

The laughter that had filled the room before suddenly evaporated as Jazz interrupted Sam with a very loud "SHHHHHHHHHHH!"

Then, whispering he said, "I don't want

Dad to know about this. I will work it out. One way or another, they've got to let me graduate. I paid for the cap and gown already. But I really don't want to disappoint Dad. He still says he will be there even if he has to ride in an ambulance."

"I know. I know. I am just really worried about you and everyone says that..." Sam stopped and looked at Jazz with deep concern; she wanted to let him know others knew what was happening.

"Well, just you no never mind what everyone says. Everyone don't know everything. So now you keep on studying. I have some sleep to catch up on. I did want you to know Miss Mary was here visiting with dad and he looks like he is really having a good time," Jazz said.

"Oh, that's wonderful. I won't bother them; I just hope she can cheer him up some. I worry about him Jazz, I'm sure you do too. Aunt Inez stopped by for a few minutes with the children today on their way to Atlanta. Uncle Carl stayed in the car. Guess we both know why," Sam said.

They looked at each other in disgust over Uncle Carl's drinking problem. Then, they both shook their heads back and forth as if to say, "What a shame."

"Dad really enjoyed seeing her and the children," Sam explained. "Aunt Inez said she was going to stop by The Store to see you. Did she?"

"She did, I really liked the fact that it was only for a minute," he confessed.

Jazz got up and reached to pick up Sam's empty glass. He started for the door, and then turned around.

"Oh, almost forgot, did you hear what happened to Doc today at The Store?" said Jazz with a concerned, surprised look on his face. They were interrupted by the ringing sound of the telephone which seemed to be continuously for Sam. Even now — at 11:15 p.m. at night — the call was for her. Sarah would have never allowed anyone to answer the phone after 9 p.m.

"Oops, sorry. Have to go. It's for me," Sam said.

Jazz was glad he and his sister had a chance to talk, even if just for a few minutes. Although they were brother and sister, they were very different. Sam acted a lot like their outgoing, carefree dad. Jazz was more shy and conservative, like their mother, though he was starting to look more and more like a young version of Robert.

As Jazz left her room with both empty glasses, he thought about how life could be compared to a full glass of tea at the beginning of your life. Then things happened, time and age, and little by little the glass became less full until it was finally empty.

Conner and Matilda's glasses were chocked full to the brim. They were very young. His glass was only a little bit less than full as was

Sam's glass. His father's glass was almost drained. His mother's glass was gone. Thinking about being gone, he rushed out to Miss Mary's car to retrieve the leftovers and placed the plates in the refrigerator.

That night, he was exhausted. His day had been jam-packed with ups and downs. Jazz laid in bed hearing the soft, sweet voices of Miss Mary and his dad. Suddenly, he heard the gentle rain coming down, pinging on the tin roof. He did not know what tomorrow would bring. Yet, the combination of these two comforting sounds made him fall into a deep peaceful sleep he had not known since his mother was alive. Jazz needed his rest to face what was ahead for him.

CHAPTER FOURTEEN

ABOUT A MONTH LATER, Jazz could hear each name being slowly called. "John Michael Caine."

It was a hot, steamy day in May. Even though the names sounded from a distance, they were only coming from a few feet away. Jazz knew each name; he had such a long history with them all.

Jazz and John used to go down to the Manicar River to see which one of them could skip stones the farthest. He dreamed of being on a boat on this river that came from the mountains, meandered all the way down to Augusta and eventually flowed into the Savannah River.

"Hubert T. Farnsworth."

Hubert and Jazz, on long summer nights when they were growing up, would try to catch fireflies to put in a glass jar. This was their idea of a flashlight without batteries.

"Marsha Jean Hollingsworth."

Jazz had always idealized her, especially

now. He would not be graduating without her honesty and integrity. He loved her, but she would be leaving.

Earlier that fine Saturday morning, when everyone had been arriving at graduation, Jazz spotted Marsha Jean in the parking lot. She looked so beautiful. Her hair glowed magnificently in the morning sunlight.

Jazz waited until her fan club moved on into the building. He still savored each brief but extremely meaningful conversation. The love smitten young man had tried to call her a million times since she had given him her numbers, but all of her numbers stayed busy constantly or she was surrounded by what Jazz called the beautiful people, the in crowd.

Surely she would have called him, if this special event had already passed. As always, she spoke first and carried the conversation.

"Hey, Jes-abe. How ya doing? Can you believe this? We are graduating today!"

"Listen, I really wanted to thank you for what you did. It meant a lot to me," Jazz said, as his heart pounded so loudly he was afraid she would hear it.

"Hey, no problem. What are friends for? We have been friends for quite sometime now," Marsha Jean said. "I couldn't let that bully keep my Sweet Jes-abe from wearing a funny dress and hat with a tassel that looks like a big strand of hair hanging off the side."

They both laughed as Marsha Jean pointed at Jazz's graduation gown and then gently tossed his tassel from one side to the other. Jazz felt his face begin to flush and turn red. The words "My Sweet Jes-abe" would ring eternally in his ears.

As he hung his head down, he reached to zip up his gown. Once zipped completely up their hands slightly touched then the love of his life began to straighten his collar. She was his first love indeed.

In this moment of elation, Jazz suddenly felt his heart hit the pavement. Oh, how he wished his mother was there to see this glorious day. He ached for Sarah to straighten his clothes as only a loving mother can do. Jazz wanted his mother to be proud because he was the first one in the family to graduate from high school.

"Well... I wouldn't be here if you hadn't done what you did. Thank you isn't enough," Jazz gushed.

Someone had spray painted the initials JT on Jazz's locker in the main school hall as well as on his gym locker. The principal called Jazz and several other boys into the office right after the initials were found. The students' graduation would be dependent upon whether or not they were involved in this vandalistic act. A full investigation was carried out.

However, as soon as Marsha Jean found out, she did a little investigative work on her own. Once she had proof, she went to the principal and explained Jazz was at work that afternoon. The time clock at The Store could verify this. The act occurred on a Saturday as best the principal could tell.

However, Joshua Taylor, the school bully, had been in Wal-Mart earlier that day and bought the same color of bright orange spray paint. It just happened to be the last can. No other shipments had arrived since his purchase. All the other cans of paint that The Store received in that color were purchased by the transportation department. The records in The Store could prove it.

Joshua had even had the nerve to go over to Marsha Jean at the jewelry counter and show it to her.

"We're graduating in a few weeks, but not all of us will get a chance to walk across that stage," Joshua boldly told her.

When she asked him what he meant, he laughed with a devilish look in his eyes.

"You'll see. They'll all see. And only I will know," the bully said.

To close the case, The Store video cameras proved what she was saying was accurate. Joshua was clearly seen on tape purchasing the same color paint as was on the lockers.

"Oh... it was nothing," Marsha Jean said. "You would have done the same for me. Listen, I still need to talk to you about that upcoming special event, I need you to..."

At that moment her parents walked up

and began taking pictures. This abruptly ended their conversation.

Jazz wanted to tell her he was still trying to call all the numbers she had given to him to discuss their upcoming date, but her phones were always busy. To Jazz, an upcoming special event sounded like a concert in Augusta with Marsha Jean. He could not believe his ears.

He would have to think about this later. Everyone was moving into the school gym for graduation. Jazz indeed had to pinch himself. He truly believed he was dreaming. The gym looked great filled with balloons and colorful decorations, just as he imagined it would look.

Mrs. Bentley as usual had done a great job decorating. The day had finally come as he heard each graduate's name being called one by one.

"Jesabe Washington Tyler!"

To him, his name resounded throughout The Woods. With all the pride he could possibly have, he stood ten feet tall as he walked across the stage. Each graduate had been instructed to stop at a certain point to have their picture taken with the principal as he handed them their diploma. Out of the corner of his eye, he could see his father and sister laughing with joy while waving at him.

Robert's health was slowly getting worse, but today he was here to share in this important moment. This was one father who would not have missed his son's graduation for anything. Sitting right next to his father was Miss Mary. What a saint, he thought. Some of his Wal-Mart family were able to make it as well.

The camera flashed and Jazz could not see for a moment. He was unsure if this was because of the sudden bright light or because he was overcome with tears of joy. His graduation day had finally arrived and now the moment was fleeting like the flashbulb.

Quickly, Vera recited a poem that she had written for this occasion. She was followed by the Reverend Bentley giving a closing prayer that invoked one's spirit similar to an altar call.

After graduation, everyone chatted with excitement about where they would be attending school in the fall. Jazz just listened and absorbed this unbelievable day. He knew he would be in Cumberland Woods, but thoughts of being at The Store comforted him. Jazz was surrounded by his family, friends, and all the love that can come with such a special time in one's life. His happiness was indeed momentary.

Mr. Johnston was making his way across the gym to see him. Jazz beamed with pride, knowing he was indeed a high school graduate at last. He was also elated that he had 100 percent perfect attendance for 13 years, from kindergarten through the twelfth grade. He had a certificate to prove it. Surely, Mr. Johnston was coming to congratulate and tell him how proud he was of him.

"Jazz, I'm sorry to tell you this but we have been a little short of help today over at The

Store. I really need you to leave now and go to back to work," Mr. Johnston said with a solemn look on his face.

His words shattered the moment like a fire in a paper mill. Mr. Johnston could at least have said: "Congratulations!" or something appropriate for this day of all days.

"I'll go," Jazz stated without emotion.

Mr. Johnston turned, vanishing into the crowd, as if his mission had been accomplished.

Jazz slowly took off his graduation robe as if he were laying aside his childhood. He was an adult now in the world of grown ups. Casually, he hugged his father, Sam and then Miss Mary, who broke the silence.

"Now, don't you go paying him any mind. I certainly don't. Let's not allow him to spoil our good time," proclaimed Miss Mary. They all smiled and laughed. This little comment seemed to help lighten the crushing moment for Jazz.

"You go take your dad and Sam home now. I'll meet you back at The Store and we will continue this party later I will assure you," Miss Mary said. She had a way about her that would put a smile on a dead man's face.

Upon his return, Jazz entered the back door. He wanted to walk through The Store he loved so much. The sweet aroma wafting from the bakery lightened his load. Nobody could make fresh bread smell as good as Miss Vera. Did this mean she was back? That would be great news. It would almost make up for the abrupt interruption imposed on him from Mr. Johnston's announcement.

He did not mind working and he certainly did not mind being at The Store, it was just the way Mr. Johnston had searched him out to demand he return to his job that he did not appreciate.

Approaching the bakery, Jazz could see someone working in that department and although her back was to Jazz it looked like Miss Vera.

"Why Miss Vera you are a sight for sore eyes indeed," he blurted out in unbelievable excitement. He did not realize he could speak so loudly. As the woman turned around he could see that it was not Miss Vera.

"I am not Vera. I wish everyone would stop calling me that," the woman said. Jazz did not know who this woman was but he did think she resembled Miss Vera.

"Sorry," Jazz said.

He was terribly embarrassed. This tall, slightly overweight, dark-haired woman sounded like she was offended to be called Miss Vera. Even though Jazz did not know who she was, he felt like telling her she should be honored that anyone would compare her to Miss Vera.

He briefly put his hands in his pockets and began straighten his vest as if he were shaking off any bad feelings this woman gave him. Suddenly, someone grabbed Jazz's right arm spinning him around as if he were on a ride at the county fair.

CHAPTER FIFTEEN

"JAZZ, HOW'VE YOU BEEN? I haven't seen you since that Saturday in April out in the parking lot when I was so upset," Miss Vera shouted. Her loud booming voice was never so loud or so booming. Yet, Jazz did not care. He was truly thrilled to see her. Now, he was speechless.

"Got a minute?"

Jazz shook his head wildly in agreement, but in his heart he knew he really needed to get to work. Still he wanted just a minute with Miss Vera to find out what had happened. Questions were swirling around in his head like a tornado.

He knew he would never ask Miss Vera anything. He would just say he missed her and was glad to have her back at The Store.

"Come on back, Jazz. I 've got something for you," Miss Vera motioned.

Jazz gladly followed her thinking it was a chicken leg. Sometimes, Miss Vera cooked too many legs on purpose knowing how much Jazz loved them. She knew they reminded him of his mother's cooking. When they got back into the kitchen, the phone was ringing. Miss Vera motioned for Jazz to have a seat.

"Take a load off whilst I answer this call," she said, pointing to a tiny table with two chairs. "Hey Sarah! Thanks... I am thrilled to be back! Well ... it all started when a customer came in and he was visiting some relatives here in The Woods. Yeah, you know, the Harpers. Anywho, he was a traveling salesman 'bout to get hitched up to some gal he met over in Augusta. I don't rightly recollect his name right now, but I hope I never see him again," Miss Vera explained in detail. Jazz tried to act like he wasn't paying any attention, but he was listening intently.

The other person on the line must have been talking because Miss Vera was quiet for a few moments. Out of the corner of his eye, he caught a glimpse of a beautiful cake.

"Oh yeah, Marsha Jean and I both were accused of being in on it. That's why that private investigator was sent all the way over here from Augusta to check us out. No, no, no... he was not from some corporate office at Wal-Mart, now you know The Store don't operate like that."

Jazz continued to listen as he saw the cake had a big picture on it. The box the cake was in was closed so he could not see it very well but he wanted to. He thought it must be for a party at Marsha Jean's house to celebrate her graduation.

"Oh yeah. But we've been cleared now of all wrong doing," Miss Vera boasted. "See Mr. Johnston told both of us that he thought it would be best if Marsha Jean and I went home until our names were no longer involved in this mess. He thought it would be best for everyone concerned. He was right. We still got paid but we couldn't come to work. All in all, it turned out to be a good deal for everyone. Well, almost everyone, see this guy's fiancé almost died. Said she's still in the hospital from what he did to her and he tried to blame it on us."

Jazz stopped thinking about everything except what Miss Vera was saying. How could his beautiful Marsha Jean could even be remotely involved in anything shady. This just could not be.

"Well, this guy claims he purchased an engagement ring from Marsha Jean. Then, he came over here to the bakery department and got a cupcake. He said both Marsha Jean and I encouraged him to ask his fiancé to marry him and then give her a cupcake that had the ring hidden in it," Miss Vera explained.

Jazz chuckled — what a silly thing to do.

"Oh yeah. Lord knows I would've never done anything like that. That's the most ridiculous thing I have ever heard of. Unfortunately, the fiancé swallowed the ring and it got caught in her windpipe. This all happened over in Augusta in a public restaurant. Luckily, there was a doctor sitting nearby who knew how to do the "Hymliker" thing or whatever it's called that gets out what you're choking on.

"Still they say she had to have surgery to repair her throat and vocal cords due to the scratches. No... she can't talk yet, but I hear the doctors say she will be just fine in a couple of weeks. Can you imagine how horrible that would be?

"No, didn't seem to affect Marsha Jean though. You know her daddy's a big executive in that legal thing. You know they sell legal policies. Yeah, what I understand it's like an HMO except with attorneys. She had their attorney call this man's lawyer and got everything straightened out for both of us. I got me a policy while all this mess was going on. Best thing I could've done. Saved me a bunch of money, 'cause I needed to talk to an attorney on a daily basis. With this policy that was no problem," Miss Vera shared.

Jazz knew he had heard enough and this answered a lot of questions for him. It was time for him to go to the parking lot and start collecting carts before Mr. Johnston found him. Shoppers needed Jazz.

As he stood up and began to straighten his orange safety vest, he heard footsteps coming.

"Oh yeah, you bet I wrote a poem about this. Wanna hear it? Oops, no. Gotta run," Miss Vera said rather quickly.

She slammed the phone down on the wall receiver because she too heard the booming noise of what sounded like a giant's steps echoing down a castle's corridor.

"Jazz, what's taking so long? Graduation has been over for at least 30 minutes," questioned Mr. Johnston.

Jazz knew from experience just to smile, shake his head in agreement and not to say anything. He wondered how Mr. and Mrs. Johnston had ever met. Mrs. Johnston was one of Jazz's favorite teachers. She always gave everybody a chance and listened when they had something to contribute. He thought that the two of them were very different, very different indeed.

Before Mr. Johnston could continue, Miss Vera intervened.

"Good to be back at work, Mr. Johnston. Hope you don't mind but I need Jazz to help me get this cake out to the parking lot. Real important that I don't drop it and I need someone who is big and strong to help me out," Miss Vera said.

Miss Vera pointed to the cake Jazz had been gleefully eyeing. He just knew in his heart this was a very special cake for a unique event. Miss Vera knew Mr. Johnston would not help. He would have something else to do that he thought was much more important than transporting a "confectionary work of art" as Miss Vera would often refer to her pastries.

"Oh, I see. Carry on," Mr. Johnston said as he flicked his hand up into the air and briskly sauntered away. After he was gone, Jazz and Miss Vera laughed heartily.

"Oh, I see. Carry on," mocked Miss Vera in a high-pitched childlike voice. Jazz continued to laugh as he began to leave the kitchen; he had to get to work.

Miss Vera continued, "Now, wait just a minute. Not so quick young man. I meant what I said. I need some help to get this monster-sized cake out of here."

"No problem. I just thought that..."

Miss Vera interrupted, "I know what you thought; you thought I was making all of that up to save your hide. Well, I always tell the truth, might stretch it a little but as I always say — truth is like a rubber band. No matter how much you stretch it, it will always come back and pop you on the hand."

This rhyme came out of Miss Vera like a Top 40 hit song. Jazz smiled not knowing exactly what she meant, but he found it amusing at any rate.

"Now, you pick up that end by sliding both hands under the box. Let's go out the front door and head toward the lawn and garden department," Miss Vera instructed.

Everyone at The Store gave directions according to where the department was located. Whoever was coming to pick up the cake must have been parked in that area. As they passed the front of the bakery that woman was standing there that Jazz thought was Miss Vera.

"Say hello to Tera, my sister. She has moved down here to be with me awhile, so I put her to work. She needed a job." Then, Miss Vera whispered: "She's going through a d-i-v-o-r-c-e, getting an Assurance Plan attorney with a 25 percent discount," Miss Vera said with a smile.

"Nice to meet you, Tera," Jazz said. He knew she was not from around here, but now that he knew the connection he was relieved. Folks in Hope County often took awhile to warm up to strangers until they knew them or someone in the area claimed to be their kin.

"Yeah, you too," Tera said loudly without meaning while she flipped the big hot potato wedges into the bin to cool down before selling them.

The sound of the potatoes sizzling combined with the smell of fresh cooked ones made Jazz remember he had not had anything to eat or drink since yesterday.

Carefully, Miss Vera and Jazz carried the enormous art work out the front door. As they headed toward the lawn and garden department, he could see there were balloons tied to the furniture outside. Mr. Johnston was always doing something to entice customers to notice the outdoor items.

As Jazz got closer though he realized this was no ordinary Saturday Sale.

CHAPTER SIXTEEN

JAZZ'S THOUGHTS momentarily returned to his father as he said a silent prayer under his breath for him.

Immediately following graduation, Jazz took Robert and Sam back home. Robert was exhausted from the experience. His once strong and seemingly indestructible body was now frail.

When Jazz pulled into the driveway and halted the car, what he saw made his heart almost stop. Robert had reclined his seat for the five minute ride and his mouth was gaping open. Jazz thought his father was dead.

"Dad! Dad!" cried Jazz while Sam leaned over from the back seat with a look of horror on her face.

Suddenly, Robert stirred from a deep sleep and proclaimed, "What is all of the commotion? Oh. I see, we're back home — safe and sound. You are such a good driver, son. Well... I guess this is as good a time as any. Jazz, I just want you to know how very proud your mother and I are of you. I want you to have this. It was your mother's, and your great-grandfather's."

Jazz reached out his hand as his father placed decades of memories and stories in his young hand. This was his mother's prize possession. On lonely nights when Sarah found her world to be filled with unbearable hardships, she would go into her bedroom and pull out a metal box with a lock on it.

Sarah hid the tiny key in a little pocket she had sewn into her bra. She said this way she could always remember she had come from somewhere and people loved her, even if they were dead. They may have taken the land, but they could not take her memories or her heart.

Jazz and Sam both remembered times when their mother thought they were asleep. She would go and get this sacred timepiece for solace. As far as monetary value, Jazz didn't believe there was any, but the sentimental value was immeasurable. Jazz now had a watch and he would carry it always in his pocket.

"SURPRISE!" Miss Mary screamed and it seemed like the whole town yelled with her. It was a graduation party for the school. Graduates began pouring out of each others' cars while moms and dads were taking pictures. Some still had their graduation robes on; others were starting to take the gowns off. All the graduates were gathering there in the outdoors area, except Carlton Phillips and Genesis Hartley— who were dead — and Matthew Lumpkin — who was in the hospital. Everyone secretly was glad that Joshua was not there; he always created trouble. Folks from all over Cumberland Woods were turning out. Someone had even brought up a CD player from the electronics department and was playing some songs that had been hits during the school year. The balloons waving in the light May breeze were the school colors.

Mr. Johnston must have been joshing him to get him to come back to The Store on his day off.

"Miss Mary, how… why…. what is this?" As usual Jazz did not know what to say; he was overcome with happiness.

"This is your graduation party. I told you that we would celebrate later. Well, this is later," Miss Mary said, laughing loud and hearty.

Jazz thought she always had a way of making things turn out all right.

Fresh All-American brand hamburgers were cooking on the grills. Mr. Thigpen was flipping the half-done sizzling patties.

"Now, watch out for the little ones' hands everyone. These grills are really hot," he warned.

Mr. Thigpen was a great person to put in charge because he was concerned about safety, with all of his years of experience with saws and repairs.

"All right now. Let's all have a good time and make some noise. The line for the vittles starts over here and these three blue coolers are full of all kinds of -- you guessed it -- delicious Wal-Mart drinks," Miss Mary exclaimed.

Jazz checked and sure enough there was plenty of Sam's Choice grape soda, his favorite. Indeed, this was a party. He thought there could have been no better place on Earth than to have a party than here.

There were grills, chairs, even tables with umbrellas. Jazz wondered how Miss Mary was able to pull this off with Mr. Johnston.

He really did not care right now though; Marsha Jean was waving at him and walking over to speak. Jazz knew she wanted to discuss their date, whenever it was.

"Hey Jes-abe. Remember that time we were swinging over at the Clayton's pond?" They both giggled, with Marsha Jean's louder than his.

"I'm… I'm still sorry about that," Jazz said as he blushed.

That day long ago Marsha Jean was sitting on top of a tire swing. As he pushed her to make her go out farther, she was flung out over the pond just as the rope broke loose from the tree.

"That's okay. It was really hot that day, so it helped to cool me down. Only thing was I had to go home and explain to my folks why I was soaked from head to toe when I was supposed to be just swinging and picking up jacks with my friends," she said with a smile.

Jazz had a lot of fond memories with Marsha Jean. He had no idea she even remotely remembered any of the events he treasured. He thought that life could never get any better than this moment. This was his perfect vision of what heaven must be like.

Jazz's thoughts were interrupted when a 1973 Red Dodge Challenger with headers came driving up real fast. Everyone stopped what they were doing. The sound of squealing tires against the asphalt and then the smell of burning rubber captured the party goers attention. The car drove right up to the celebration.

Suddenly, the happy festive mood changed.

He got out of the car screaming and looking for a fight. "I'm a gonna getcha, Boy. You and ya goody, goody two shoes attitude. You had no right to tell the principal it was me that spray painted those lockers and stole that money out of the coach's desk drawer," Joshua T. Taylor hollered.

He believed Jazz had ratted him out and this was why he was not able to participate in the graduation ceremony that morning.

Getting closer, Joshua continued to shout, "I call you out right now. My Paw said me and you have a score to settle, you settle like men. I call you out right now. Right here, right now. Let's me and you go back into The Woods and settle this thing right now."

Joshua was mad, real mad. Folks knew he

and his whole entire clan could get riled up real easy. Only problem was Joshua wasn't real smart. Jazz was a great deal smarter, just not physically quick on his feet.

Jazz really did not know what to do. There was talk in The Woods that several hunting accidents had occurred on the Taylor land that were not really accidents. Folks in general knew better than to mess with the Taylors.

"I don't know what you're talking about! I did not..." Jazz stumbled over his words like a two-year-old toddler attempting to walk the length of a football field without falling down.

Joshua was in his face, pushing Jazz in the chest with his pointed index finger.

"Yes, you do, Boy. Yes, you and God almighty do know what I am talking about," Joshua continued.

Once the name of God entered into the discussion Miss Mary became involved.

"Now, Josh let's not be bringing down the name of God here, we are having a celebration and you graduated today, too. Come on over here and have a hamburger, son. You and I both know your mother is a fine Sunday School teacher who likes to use you and your brother in her Sunday morning illustrations," she reminded him.

The party goers all seemed to chuckle lightly over Miss Mary's comments because she was right.

"'Cepting I don't believe this will be one

story she is gonna be able to use. All right now, everybody turn the music back up and let's continue to celebrate," Miss Mary declared.

Josh put his head down so no one could see the fire of hatred glowing in his eyes. Miss Mary put her hand on his shoulder and guided him over to the grill like a second grader. She got him something to eat and drink then helped him find a seat.

The Reverend Bentley came walking up to Miss Mary. "Sister Carter, so sorry to be late for this wonderful celebration," he said. "I know you have worked hard to pull everything together for the graduates, but I couldn't help it. I would have been here sooner, but I was down in Augusta at the hospital. It concerns you, but we can discuss it a little later."

The preacher talked with desperation in his voice as he towered over Miss Mary. The two of them had a great deal of history together, the kind that binds deep close friendships.

Jazz wondered what the problem was and who was in the hospital. Then his mind briefly thought about happier times when the Reverend Bentley and Robert would reminisce about their days as soldiers when they were based over at Fort Gordon. Jazz liked to hear them talk and believed Army life must knit close ties between people that even family cannot understand.

Miss Mary was glad to see the preacher. "Now, don't worry about it. You have come at the perfect time. Trust me… we need a prayer."

Then, she turned to the graduates and their families. "All right now, I need everybody's attention. Yeah, so hush up now. The Reverend Bentley's going to give a fine celebration word and a prayer to bless you young folks on your road of life today and eternally."

The Reverend Bentley chuckled. "Well, thank you, Sister Carter, I believe you just said it all."

Everyone seemed to be pleased at this moment, except of course, Joshua who never seemed to be at peace with anything in his life. Jazz thought about what his dad always said, "You have to choose to be happy."

Growing up, Jazz remembered thinking this was silly. Who would not choose to be happy? Now, he knew. Joshua was one of those folks who stirred up constant conflict.

"Let's bow our heads to honor a most, merciful God on this blessed occasion," the Reverend Bentley stood up tall and declared.

The pastor paused for a moment until only the sound of birds chirping in the background was audible. Then, he raised both of his hands to the heavens and began.

"Oh God, thank you for allowing these young folks to learn and grow up here in these beautiful Woods that you have given to us. Let them recall all of their childhood memories of good ethical standards and fine morals that this community has shown them. Let them choose the righteous path of God as they go out into the world. Never let them forget that Jesus was their most merciful Savior and died for their sins so that they may have eternal life.

"No matter where their path leads them tomorrow, help them to always remember where they came from and to honor God, their families, this community as well as this great country, America! Bless and protect these children whom we are all very proud of for each of their accomplishments, these precious lambs of God, these Cumberland Woods' children that we have dedicated to you Almighty God. In Jesus' Name we all say A-MEN," he finished.

The preacher had a way about him that could rival any television evangelist. He knew how to punctuate each word so a tingle went up your spine while a tear or two rolled down your face at any moment. He was a true man of God.

A calm, peace returned to the party, but not for long.

All the way on the other side of the parking lot, someone was coming toward them — rushing for them. Jazz squinted to see who it was, but the glare from the hot pavement and car windshields seemed to make it impossible to see. Then, he heard the person yelling his name very loudly:

"JAZZ! JAZZ! Son, what is your problem? What in Heaven's name is going on here? Why... did Miss Mary put you up to this? Son, I promise you that someday you are going to lose your job following after that woman's words!"

Jazz recognized the voice and the face at the same time — Mr. Johnston.

"Mr. Johnston, this was all my idea. I just thought…" Miss Mary was trying to intervene with what seemed like the devil himself. Apparently, he did not know about any of this.

"THOUGHT? Thought? I don't recall asking you to think," Mr. Johnston yelled.

Oh no… to shame Miss Mary in front of the town was not a good idea thought Jazz. Mr. Johnston's throat was going to hurt tomorrow from all that screaming he had just been doing.

They both stepped off to the side. The conversation went on for several minutes with Miss Mary and Mr. Johnston having a very serious word exchange that was getting warmer by the second.

She pleaded with him to listen. The Greeter would not go against the management, but originally another supervisor was scheduled to work that day. Miss Mary had spoken with him and he had no problem with the school's graduation party being there.

When she saw Mr. Johnston at graduation, he did not give her a chance to talk and, even so, Miss Mary assumed the managers had discussed it. If there was a problem, surely someone would have spoken to her.

Miss Mary was now explaining that she wanted to do something nice for the graduates, especially since Jazz and Marsha Jean were store employees. Further, this would be the last time the entire class would be together.

Miss Mary knew that for various reasons the graduates did not have any other place to go. Also, she thought it would be good for The Store. With a look of shock on his face, Mr. Johnston stopped and replied, "Well, now... how is that?"

Miss Mary explained she knew every Saturday he tried to bring customers attention to the lawn and garden department. Surely, the smell of fresh, sizzling hamburgers and top hits playing on a featured sale item would boost sales.

Mr. Johnston shook his head in disagreement and emphatically told her, "For your sake, you better hope it increases sales today."

He then turned and pointed at Jazz. "Now as for you young man, I am very..."

"Wait just a minute," someone in the crowd interrupted as they made their way over to Mr. Johnston.

CHAPTER SEVENTEEN

"SORRY TO BARGE IN on your conversation, but I am sure you were about to say how very pleased you are with Jazz today because you need to tell him and all of the graduates CONGRATULATIONS!" Mrs. Johnston said to her soul mate in a matter-of-fact school teacher voice.

Then, she clasped her long, slim fingers together in front of her and stood up straight. "Further, honey, I know you want to thank all of the graduates as well as their parents for shopping at their local Wal-Mart and remember your store has a photography studio to take lovely portraits of the graduates and their families as well as a wide selection of graduation gifts," his wife continued. "Isn't that what you were going to say?"

Coming from Mrs. Johnston it was well received. The timing of her arrival could not have been better.

Mr. Johnston cleared his voice and announced, "Yes, I agree with everything Mrs.

Johnston just said. I hope everyone has a good time and remember to shop here at your local Wal-Mart. Thank you! Now Jazz..."

Everyone forgot what had happened. They returned to eating and reminiscing. The graduates had gone to school together all of their lives; this was a happy as well as sad occasion. They had ties to one another, often closer than their own family.

Mrs. Johnston again interrupted her husband, "Did I tell you Jazz wrote a wonderful English paper entitled 'Why I like Working at Wal-Mart?'"

Mr. Johnston shook his head.

The instructor continued as if she were giving an explanation on a class assignment: "Part of the reason was you, Mr. Johnston. Believe it or not!" The Store manager remained silent, as if waiting for his final directions.

Next, Mrs. Johnston gave Jazz his marching orders. "Jazz, give me your safety vest and I will go collect buggies for The Store. You stay here and enjoy the party as long as you like," she said.

By then, she already had the vest off of Jazz and was wearing it. With that command, Mrs. Johnston — who looked like the typical school teacher — held up her hand to stop traffic and proceeded across the parking lot to begin her personal mission. Mr. Johnston followed her with admiration in his eyes.

Jazz was about to follow her and resume his job when he felt a hand on his shoulder.

"All right Mr. Goody," Joshua said in a snide tone. "I've had my five burgers and six sodas and now I'm ready to even the score. My Paw said men in our family don't git mad they's git even."

Everybody usually looked the other way when it came to Joshua because the folks in The Woods knew something was wrong with him. He could hurt you.

Often, people said Joshua's parents must have met at a family reunion. They could have been related, because his parents had the same last name before they got married and both sons acted like they had been touched in the head. It was people like the Taylors that gave southerners a bad name.

Jazz could feel his face getting hot and his palms starting to sweat. He had never been in a real fight before. His main concern was for the family heirloom he was carrying in his right back pocket. If he pulled it out now it could get broken, if he fell backwards on the ground it could get crushed.

He prayed someone would help him fast as Joshua forcefully grabbed him and twisted up the front of his work shirt. Joshua pulled back his other hand and made a tight fist that was sure to knock out at least three or four of Jazz's front pearly whites. Jazz braced himself.

"STOP NOW! Stop it right this second!" Jazz had already closed his eyes waiting to see stars circling his head for the next few days when the voice of an angel halted this tear down.

"I'm the one that told the Principal about the orange spray paint," Marsha Jean declared as one of her dainty fingers pointed at The Store. "You came in on a Saturday back in March and stomped up to my counter — do you remember what you said?"

Marsha Jean was unstoppable — like a freight train on its way to McCormick, South Carolina, to deliver goods on a deadline.

Joshua was not fast enough to say anything, but he did let Jazz go while he shook his head no. Everyone could tell he was stunned by her beauty and the fact she was actually talking to him.

The Jewelry Goddess continued while she rolled her head back and forth simultaneously throwing her right arm up in the air for illustration. "Well, I'm going to tell you what you said. 'We're graduating in a few weeks, but not all of us will get a chance to walk across that stage.'

"Then, I asked you what you meant by that. You starting walking away from the counter saying: 'You'll see. They'll all see. And only I will know.' Yeah, well we did see and now we all know you were the one that did not get a chance to walk across that stage! You tried to set Jes-abe up by spraying his locker with those initials of JT on it, but it didn't work.

"Not only that, but the video cameras in The Store show you were the one who bought the last and only can of paint in that color. As far as

you coming around here making threats to us --
yes I said us because when you make threats to
Jes-abe, you are making threats at me and all of
us here today."

The good folks of Cumberland Woods were
tired of Joshua Taylor pushing them around.

"Oh yeah," Josh challenged, coiled like a
copperhead snake ready to strike. "So what are
you, Miss Rich Girl, going to do about it?"

"For starters on Monday morning, I am
going to call my law firm," Marsha Jean said as
she pulled out her blue glowing cellular phone
and stuck it in Joshua's face.

"We ain't got no attorneys in this county
and you know it Marsha Jean. You are full of b-o-
l-o-a-n-e," Joshua proudly claimed.

Truth be know, Joshua would not have
graduated with a high school diploma even if he
had walked across the stage. More than likely, he
would have received a certificate of attendance.
He was just not that smart.

"I have access to 2,700 attorneys across the
country. I am going to call one of them and Sheriff
Rowe to let 'um know if anything happens to me
or Jazz the police need to be knocking on your
door. Everyone here is a witness to Joshua T.'s
threats!"

Joshua started walking backward to his
car, slithering away like the snake he was.
Everyone started to applaud Marsha Jean while
they hoped Joshua went back into The Woods and

crawled under that rock he came out from.

Right when Joshua was about to get into his car, Marsha Jean yelled out one last nail for his coffin.

"Oh yeah, by the way Joshua... everyone here today heard that little comment about you taking money out of coach's desk drawer," she said. The laughter could have been heard all the way down the Manicar River clean to Augusta.

Another cheer went up for Marsha Jean. "Okay... Okay... now quiet down. I am not joking — I am calling my law firm on Monday as well as the Sheriff to let them know what just happened. Thanks, but no applause was necessary," Marsha Jean said.

At that precise moment, her phone rang. Marsha Jean stuck one of her beautiful, dainty fingers in her ear and meandered away from the party to have a private conversation.

Just then Sam casually walked up with an envelope in her hand. "Hey Jazz. This is for you. Sorry, I'm a little late, but I wanted to wait till Dad ate something and then fell asleep to walk over even though that didn't take long at all."

Jazz knew that it was only a five-minute walk through The Woods so he figured his dad must have been slap worn out from graduation.

"Who's staying with Dad?" Jazz looked worried.

"Oh, don't worry. Mrs. Marlene Turnbow stopped by to drop off some dog food. She said she would just sit on the front porch and visit with Wal-do until I returned. She doesn't mind keeping out a listen for him," Sam said then looked around gleefully. "Well, what's been going on — did I miss anything?"

Jazz smiled and shook his head. He knew as popular as Sam was she would hear all about it momentarily.

"Go ahead, open your present," Sam said anxiously.

As he opened the Hallmark envelope, he could tell the card was not important but what was inside, the cart pusher had never seen before. He felt the moisture instantly stream down his face when he eyeballed the contents.

Jazz had to run into The Woods on the other side of The Store to keep from letting anyone see the tears of a broken-hearted young man.

CHAPTER EIGHTEEN

FOLKS WERE STARTING to leave the once in a lifetime celebration. Before they left, Miss Mary asked them to sing their school song. Marsha Jean had a beautiful voice and led them one last time. Their thoughts reflected on where they would go from here. Jazz returned in time to join in.

Some graduates would stay forever in Cumberland Woods, some by choice and some by fate. Carlton Phillips and Genesis Hartley would remain forever in The Woods, buried in the New Hope Church of God cemetery right next to the sanctuary.

They died in separate, unfortunate accidents that were not their faults. Genesis died in a car wreck with an innocent, young Christian man, while Carlton met his Maker in a hunting tragedy.

Jazz visited their graves often. Matthew Lumpkin might join Carlton and Genesis soon, if his heart transplant was not forthcoming in the immediate future.

Others would be leaving in the fall going to various technical schools and universities. By the end of the song, most were in tears for they knew nothing would ever be the same for any of them.

One by one, the graduates and their families came to tell Miss Mary thank you for all of her years of positive encouragement, unending prayers as well as the graduation party. For the most part, Evanston was a simple town with simple needs.

Miss Mary reminded each of them to be thankful to The Store, which donated the food, drinks, plates, ice, napkins and trash bags as well as the location. The parents knew where the party was going to be, but the graduating class members were not told so that this would be a surprise.

After the ceremony, the students were told by their parents they had to stop by The Store for various reasons. This was believable to the graduates, as well as understandable. Jazz had noticed no matter where he was, most conversations included a discussion about the next visit to Wal-Mart and what would be purchased.

The Greeter had cooked half a dozen hummingbird cakes and was asking for any donation for each slice to help out Matthew with his transplant surgery. Although the Wal-Mart graduation cake was beautiful, everybody wanted a slice of both cakes.

Graduates were eager to help, especially one of their own classmates. Matthew had been too sick to come to graduation but his parents were there and his mother was allowed to march in the line to receive his diploma.

Everyone got emotional when Matthew's mother walked across the stage. The audience as a whole began shedding tears when Carlton Phillips's mother, Sabrina, and Genesis Hartley's father, Anthony, and mother, Paige, received their children's diplomas.

Carlton was handsome and very talented. He could play the guitar as well as draw like a professionally trained artist. Jazz would always ask Carl to help him with illustrations for school projects because the assignments would turn out perfect.

Carl was also an expert with rifle presentation and the commander of his ROTC unit. The whole town was still very upset about this tragedy so close to home. Everyone wondered what would become of the pending lawsuit.

The Reverend Anthony Hartley, the minister of The First Baptist Church, was asked to give the commencement speech and did a fine job. Jazz could tell God had anointed him with words. He knew he certainly could not have talked about Carl or Genesis. He loved both of them dearly, but he would have choked up.

In memory of the classmates who died, everyone stood for a moment of silence at the end of the ceremony. The silence was followed by a professional recording of Genesis singing: "How Could I Ask For More?" by Cindy Morgan.

While the song played, the Reverend Hartley showed a slide presentation of all of the graduates as babies and different pictures of them growing up at school as well as around town — school trips to Augusta and Six Flags in Atlanta. Special pictures brought back fond, yet emotionally charged memories.

While the song played, Jazz thought about his mother tucking him in to sleep at night and his father holding his hand as they walked down those back country dirt roads. He reflected on times when his friend Hubert and he used to catch fireflies together. Genesis's melody had been this graduating class's theme song which told a whole story that Jazz felt was his life.

The words of the song were quite moving. There was not a dry eye in the house — even Jazz fought hard to conceal his tears for the words struck close to his own heart. There were so many unanswered questions in all of their lives he thought, but especially his. He personally knew this to be true.

The slide show ended with a picture of one of the graduates in kindergarten smiling and waving goodbye in front of the school. Jazz knew it was Marsha Jean being dropped off for her first day. He knew because he had been there.

Although Genesis had died a few years ago in a car accident, Jazz thought about her daily as he listened to one of her tapes. She was very talented and sang Christian music. He often would play her songs for encouragement. Jazz heard a Christian radio station over in Augusta still played her records.

Jazz recalled his mother lovingly talking about what a sweet girl Genesis had always been growing up in the church. She was so talented and that was one of the people Sarah wanted to see when she got to heaven.

Jazz could visualize all the times he saw his mother sweeping and singing a line from an old hymn: "When we all get to heaven, what a day of rejoicing that will be." Certainly, now his mother, Carl and Genesis were together.

Sarah had been a Sunday School teacher for children for many, many years at the church up until the year before she died. She taught at least half of the town's people.

The cart pusher's thoughts came back to the present when he heard the various graduates saying goodbye. "Miss Mary, thank you. Will you take our picture? Then, I want to get a picture with you."

This was heard over and over again while the final goodbyes were being said.

Jazz had gotten himself together. He knew time was short and he would take time later to fully understand as well as appreciate the contents of the envelope.

The big cake Miss Vera had made had been cut. Now he could see it had a picture of everyone in the graduating class on it from when they were in first grade together. He walked back up just in time to hear the bad news.

"Sister Carter, looks like Matthew has made another bad turn for the worse. The doctors at the hospital say he does not have much time, maybe a day or two… a week at the most. Sorry to be the one to tell you. We must pray for God to help us by healing him or quickly send a donor heart for him. If you want to still see him alive, you better go soon."

As Reverend Bentley shared this news with Miss Mary, she went pale and for a moment looked every bit her age as she sat down in a lawn chair. Jazz kneeled down beside her.

"Are you all right?" He inquired as if sitting at the feet of his mother.

"Sure… I'm all right. I just felt like sitting down a minute, been on my feet most of the day. Just thought so many times we had lost Matthew and then a miracle happened and we got him back. I feel like he is my own child, I use to keep him during the day when he was growing up so his momma could go back to school. He was always such a sweet child, a joy to be around. I felt like he would do great things. We have lost so much with the passing of Carl and Genesis, Lord help Matthew," Miss Mary half-way mumbled, slightly throwing up her hands and glancing at the sky in praise. "Now, only God knows."

The preacher as usual interjected his profound thoughts. "Yes, indeed, only God knows.

We all have an appointment, Sister Carter, but remember 'Ye though I walk through the Valley of the Shadow of Death, I will fear no evil thy rod and thy staff they comfort me,'" he declared as he slipped his hand into his coat pocket and pulled out a small, black worn out King James Version of The Bible.

To Jazz, the passage about the "Valley of Shadow of Death" from The Lord's Prayer meant not only did God take care of people who were dying, but also the caregivers who stayed and had to walk in their shadow of death.

The reverend was always dressed in a sharp looking dark suit. This gave the appearance that he was ready to hitch folks up in marriage or bury their kin at any given time.

"'He prepareth our coming in, just as he prepareth our going out. Blessed be the name of the Lord,'" the preacher read. A few folks still standing around added an "Amen Reverend."

Miss Mary shook her head in agreement but she did not want to believe what she heard about Matthew.

"Yes, Reverend Bentley, our God is still in the business of working miracles today. I have to go visit Matthew," Miss Mary said. "Want to come with me Jazz?

"Sure, Miss Mary," Jazz eagerly replied.

Good thing the reverend went a few times a month to Augusta to visit sick folks in the hospitals, if he did not there was no telling when news about the ill would reach The Woods.

Sam was sitting in a reclining lawn chair chatting with her friends. Every now and then she would look in Jazz's direction. He figured she was getting caught up on the Joshua situation.

Marsha Jean walked over to Jazz. "Hey, Jes-abe. We still need to talk. Got a minute?"

Jazz had all the time in the world for Marsha Jean. He barely moved his head in a slow acknowledgement.

Marsha Jean continued in her beautiful, leisurely southern drawl. Jazz loved to hear her talk. "This was really neat, wasn't it? You know it was all Miss Mary; she really loves you. She wanted to do something very nice for you, and all of the graduates as well, but especially for you."

"Naww…" Jazz put his head down while shuffling his feet. He was easily embarrassed, but mustered the courage to look at her. "I need to tell you again. Thank you. You saved my rear end, twice in one day. Must be a record for Cumberland Woods," he said.

They laughed as long-time friends often do.

"No problem. Listen…" Marsha Jean placed her beautiful hand on top of Jazz's arm. He thought his heart was going to pound right out of his chest due to sheer elation. She led him over to a comfortable chair and the two of them sat down next to each other to chew the fat.

"I hope you don't mind but I asked Mr. Johnston if you and I could both have off from work the Saturday afternoon and evening of June nineteenth," she said.

Of course, there was absolutely no way Jazz would have ever minded Marsha Jean doing anything. He shook his head in excited agreement as well as disbelief — a date with the Wal-Mart Jewelry Goddess. Oh my, he wished everyone was still there and she would have asked him like it was an announcement.

"The reason I want both of us to be off the same day is...."

CHAPTER NINETEEN

AT THAT MOMENT, something came crashing down on him. His first thoughts were Joshua Taylor had come back to clobber him from behind.

He was forcefully knocked out of the chair and thrown onto the pavement. Seemed like everyone was standing around him, leaning down and asking if he was okay. But Jazz could not talk, or see.

Then, only shoes and ankles were surrounding him. Something was on top of him. He could not breathe. Had he been hit by a car or a meteor from the sky? His thoughts wandered to Marsha Jean. Was she all right?

"Okay now, on the count of three everyone grab a body part and lift. Okay… one… two… three," Mr. Thigpen directed.

"Now I can lift him by myself," Mr. Thigpen said as he lifted Jazz up to a sitting position.

He quickly related to the wrestlers on television. He was in serious pain and he had the wind knocked out of him to boot. Mr. Thigpen reached under Jazz's arms and stood him up on his feet.

"Well now, the party is over. Looks like you had a really good time Jazz, now it's time to go back to work," Mrs. Johnston said. It seemed she had come out of nowhere.

Unaware of what just happened, she began picking up his arms one at a time and placing them into his orange safety vest.

"I am here to tell you. I do not want your job; it is much more difficult than I ever imagined. The constant pushing and walking... well, I've had my exercise for the day, no... the week," Mrs. Johnston said as she began ironing out Jazz's jacket with her well-manicured hands.

"Well, all good things must come to an end. See you later Jazz, I am proud of you," she said before disappearing into the parking lot.

Jazz felt like he was in a cartoon where the character falls off a cliff and then the birds circle the injured party's head. Slowly, he started to walk across the parking lot to begin the cart gathering.

He immediately realized he needed another minute to collect his thoughts. So, he placed his hands on a table to steady himself when he heard Mr. Johnston speak.

"Jazz, you know I have been very lenient with you today. But I am not going to put up with you breaking the rules of the cart pusher's job," he said.

Mr. Johnston was referring to the rule that neither a cart pusher nor greeter could sit or lean on anything while they were on the clock.

Jazz removed his hands slowly to find out he needed to sit down for a minute. As soon as he did so, he jumped to his feet.

The watch! Oh no... surely it must have been broken from the pounding he received. He still did not know what happened. A feeling of hopelessness gripped across his chest as he slowly moved his hand into his pocket.

Oh, yes! Thank God! The precious family heirloom was saved this time. Jazz thought that just as soon as he got home he was going to put it back in the locked box for very safe keeping. He always wondered why his mother kept it locked up — now he knew.

"What's the matter Jes-abe? I thought you would be fine by now," Marsha Jean said.

Jazz knew his face indicated shock and pain. "No, I'm fine," he quickly said. "But Marsha Jean — are you okay? What happened?"

"That's just like you to be thinking about others. My Sweet Jes-abe. I'm okay. Mr. and Mrs. Clayton are here and Mrs. Clayton apparently tripped and fell right on top of you. Knocked you clean out the chair onto the pavement and then she fell on top of you to boot — seems she has hurt her knee. Mr. Clayton has gone back to get their car to take her home."

Jazz turned to hear Miss Mary trying to

encourage Mrs. Clayton to go on into Augusta and get a doctor to look at her knee.

Mrs. Clayton was protesting. "Don't need no doctor. If Doc was here though I would let him take a look," Mrs. Clayton said. "He knows all about Johnny. You know, Johnny reminds us of a young version of Sugar Pie -- honestly, the spitting image of Charles when he wore a younger set of trousers. He always did look like him... could've been our birth son.

"We are so excited about his visit. We have received and accepted several collect calls from various payphones from our dear son as he is on his journey to see us — he will be here soon enough. Don't rightly know when though, but we will bring him around to show him off. That's why we were coming to Wal-Mart. I wanted to look at a new bedspread for his room. We haven't changed it since he was 12 years old."

Miss Mary wanted desperately to do something. "Well at least let me go in and get some cream so that you can rub it on the abrasion," Miss Mary said.

"No, strange thing about it. My skin does not seem to tear when I fall down, just seems to bruise, but thanks anyway," Mrs. Clayton said.

Mr. Clayton pulled the car up just then as close as he could.

"Here comes my Sugar Pie." Mrs. Clayton said. "Now, Sugar Pie, I know that you know what is best. But I'm thinking that if Miss Mary would go over to the front entrance and get me a riding buggy that I will be just fine. You know how much I love Wal-Mart."

Jazz knew there was always a shortage of the electric carts. So Miss Mary might not be able to find one.

For once Jazz spoke up. "I'll go Mrs. Clayton."

The look on Marsha Jean's face indicated she thought this was really sweet.

In all the excitement, Jazz forgot Marsha Jean was finally asking him for a date. June the nineteenth would live in his heart forever.

He went to fulfill his job requirements without hesitation and was glad to do so. Just as he thought though, there were no electric carts at the front. He decided to take a quick run around The Store. Perhaps one had been left somewhere.

This took longer than Jazz thought but when he realized he had done all he could do, he trotted back outside. The Clayton's were still present with their overly polite mannerisms. By now the crowd around them was growing weary.

"No, Sweet Potato, I want you to be happy," Mr. Clayton said. His term of affection would turn everyone around diabetic.

"Well, Sugar Pie, you know Johnny is coming and we need to spruce up the house. Here is the list," Mrs. Clayton firmly stated. She did not want to leave without getting her shopping done. Jazz motioned at Miss Mary that there were no electric carts to be found.

Miss Mary turned into the voice of reason. "Go home now. Get some rest. Wal-Mart is always open, but you need to relax right now. This will give you something to look forward to — and perhaps you've forgotten something. Take another look around at home. I'm always forgetting something I need when I'm at The Store."

After several more minutes of debating how to get into the car and coming back to the passenger side to roll down Mrs. Clayton's window, the car engine finally started. The Royal Couple was leaving. Jazz could see them waving goodbye in unison, like windshield wipers on a stormy night.

"Now, we got to clean up," Miss Mary said and clapped her hands once together with glee. "All in all, things turned out great." Then, she whispered at Jazz, "I think Marsha Jean likes you."

Jazz stood at least ten feet tall at that moment. A big, country boy grin creeped across his face — as if he could bite into a whole row of corn at one time.

"Her parents said it was time to leave. But, she gave me her cell phone number. She thought you must have lost it since you haven't called her yet, told me to tell you to ring her later tonight so you two could finalize plans for the nineteenth of June."

"Oh wow," thought Jazz, he would call all night if he had too. He had tried for weeks, but this evening calling her was all he would do.

This was Jazz's big break, he would call her right after work — he wanted to go ahead and discuss their date. Even though it was more than a month away, he might need some new clothes — depending on where they were going. It didn't really matter to Jazz, he just did not want to look too out of place with Marsha Jean.

His thoughts were interrupted as a man got out of a truck with yellow roses in a crystal vase. He silently walked over to Miss Mary. "Are you Mary Elizabeth Carter?"

She nodded her head yes. Everyone knew Miss Mary received yellow roses the Saturday before Mother's Day, which was the next day.

"Thank you," Miss Mary said as she accepted the roses. She took the card from the flowers and without reading it, slipped it into her skirt pocket.

EARLY THAT EVENING, Miss Mary picked Jazz up at his house. He had only been off work about 30 minutes, but already he had tried to call Marsha Jean at least 50 times.

They drove into Augusta to visit with Matthew and his family. Jazz thought it might be too late — some other folks in the community said they had heard Matthew was in a coma.

"Just because a man looks like he's asleep, doesn't mean he's not listening," Miss Mary said.

Jazz thought Miss Mary had pretty good

sense, but just the same he did not want to go to see his friend like that. When they got there, Matthew was tired, but glad to see them. The visit was a good one — yet brief.

When they returned home, Miss Mary came in to visit with Robert for awhile. Jazz thought she was a saint for coming to see a man who no longer existed except in their minds.

His father, what he used to be, had faded away. Robert was replaced by a walking dead man no one could recognize, not even his children.

CHAPTER TWENTY

SATURDAY, JUNE NINETEENTH finally arrived. The day Jazz had lived for and thought would be the day to end all days.

He would indeed remember this day, but not for the reasons he thought. Sure, he was spending it with his dream girl at Marsha Jean's house, but not the way he had always imagined.

He remembered the day at The Store, right after graduation which now seemed like a decade ago — but was only last month. Miss Mary gave him Marsha Jean's phone number again. He must have called it for three days before Marsha Jean finally answered.

He recalled that painful telephone conversation, and the severe disappointment which accompanied it.

"Hey, Marsha Jean," Jazz meekly said.

"Yeah," she replied, as if she did not know who he was.

"This is Jazz."

"Oh hey, Jes-abe," the Jewelry Goddess said. "Don't have time to talk now; I got a horse-back riding lesson. I'll call you later. When is a good time?"

For once Jazz thought quickly. He had to. He had her on the phone, now what was this about?

"I got things to do too. So if you don't mind, what is going on June nineteenth?"

"Oh... okay... well, you know my sister, Stephanie, is getting married," Marsha Jean said.

Jazz mumbled, "Uh-huh..."

Everybody in three states knew Stephanie was getting hitched to one of those Assurance Legal attorneys but he did not know when nor really care.

"Well, Mama decided to have the wedding here at the house," Marsha Jean explained as rapidly as an auctioneer at a horse sale. "You know, an old-fashioned antebellum June southern traditional wedding out back behind the house in the gazebo overlooking the pond with the swans?"

Jazz had been over to the Hollingsworth house a few times and peeked through the shrubbery to see the wealthiest people in the county, perhaps the state.

"Great," he said it like he was trying to be excited for Stephanie but he wasn't really. He did not really care, at least not too much. Well, maybe a little.

"The sheriff's department said we had so

many people on the invited guest list. Lord only knows how many there will be on the uninvited list," she said with a slight giggle.

Jazz remained silent. Now he truly wanted to finish this conversation; it was driving him insane.

"So we need at least three parking attendants wearing visible clothing. Naturally, Daddy thought of you because he knew you have a safety vest. Can you come park cars and get at least two more guys to help out as well? You know all the cart pushers better than I do," she said without taking a breath.

Naturally assuming they would all jump at the chance to be at Marsha Jean's house, she continued, "Tell them ya'll need to be here no later than 4:30 on that Saturday afternoon. The wedding starts at 6 on the dot. Now, plan on staying late cause folks will need help to get out when the party is over. Also, let 'em know they need to bring an empty belly 'cause there's going to be gracious plenty of food. I have to go. Oh by the way… of course, Daddy will pay ya'll. Talk to you later, Jessabe."

She hung up before Jazz could say anything.

Needless to say, Jazz's heart was heavy. He would have been pretty happy if she had told him this the first time she said she had to talk to him. However, he had thought for too long they were going on a date.

Jazz hit rock bottom. He wished he had not

agreed to park cars, but he tried to look on the bright side of things. His father's words rang in his ears. "Son, you have to choose to be happy!"

EVEN THOUGH IT WAS ONLY 4:45 in the afternoon, he had already parked a dozen really nice, expensive cars. If nothing else, this was a great opportunity to drive cars that most folks live a lifetime dreaming about.

Suddenly he heard his name and someone rushing toward him.

"Jes-abe, I need you to dart to The Store real fast. Here's Daddy's car keys, cell phone and a credit card. Call my cell number when you get there. Ask the head butler around back and he can tell you which garage Daddy parks in. His car's a speedball," Marsha Jean spurted.

Looking as beautiful as always, Marsha Jean had come out of nowhere wearing an exquisite, long, white southern belle dress, with a big hoop skirt and a green satin sash that accentuated her trim waist. The rest of the dress was gorgeous white lace and barely off the shoulders.

But her long blonde hair was in very large rollers wrapped tightly to her head. As Jazz walked away, he was laughing out loud.

"You best hush yourself right up now, Jes-abe," She said loudly and giggled as she went running as fast as her dress would allow her to go back up to the house.

Jazz thought about how his sister sometimes rolled her hair in old soda cans because they didn't have money for curlers. Sam rationalized it out by saying cans and rollers accomplish the same goal.

While cruising down the road, Jazz took a good look at what folks with money drove.

He... yes, Jesabe Washington Tyler was driving a brand new four-seater sports BMW M3 series convertible. Jazz knew this car cost more than his parent's house.

The top was down, yet he could still enjoy the scent of brand-new leather seats. Customers at The Store often purchased different car aromas and New Car was one of the choices. He wondered why anyone would ever do that. Now he knew. That fragrance was unbelievably wonderful.

The air conditioner could be set on his face at the temperature he wanted. Not like his family car, where his sister found out that if you put a stick or a toothbrush into the vent it would keep the air blowing on you.

Things were starting to look up a little for Jazz -- imagine driving this car into the parking lot of The Store. He just knew eyes would roll.

The smile quickly faded when he thought about explaining this if Sheriff Rowe saw him in Mr. Hollingsworth's personal car with his phone and his credit card. The proverbial ice in his tea rapidly melted.

Once at Wal-Mart, he parked but no one seemed to notice. Upon entering The Store, he saw The Greeter. Jazz was shocked to see her. "Not going to the event of the year?" he said in disbelief.

"Sure am. Got a new dress and everything, but I don't get off until 5:15 p.m.," Miss Mary said.

"It's almost that time. I had to come get something for the wedding then I got to go back. Want a ride?"

"Sure do," Miss Mary said with glee. She was excited as well as very busy.

Jazz suddenly remembered he needed to call Marsha Jean. Her cell number was busy. Wouldn't you know it?

Suddenly, Mr. Clayton came rushing into The Store.

"Hey Charles. How is Diana doing? I haven't seen ya'll since she fell last month outside The Store." Miss Mary inquired. Mr. Clayton was alone and had a dazed look on his face as he kept on walking. Apparently he had no time to talk.

Miss Mary looked puzzled at Jazz. "Did you see that Mr. Clayton did not even speak?"

Jazz just shrugged his shoulders and figured Mr. Clayton had no time to talk. Neither did he. The phone was ringing now... six rings...10... 30... Jazz was afraid if he hung up he would get a busy signal for three days like he did before.

Long about 50 rings one of the maids answered the phone. He quickly told her what was going on. It was 5:15 p.m. when Marsha Jean casually answered like nothing was going on.

"Marsha Jean, it's me, Jazz!"

"Hey Jes-abe…What's going on?" Like this was just another casual conversation. Nothing ever seemed to bother her. He thought this must be the way people with money act.

"I have been trying to get a hold of you," Jazz said, frustrated. "I'm at The Store. What do you need?"

"Oh, yeah. One of the bridesmaids needs a pair of panty hose. Although she is not very big, she likes the coffee color and a 1 X-large for the size. And I need..." The phone signal died.

How could Jazz purchase a women's pair of panty hose? How could he ever explain this to the other employees?

He quickly ran to the hosiery department like an Olympic sprinter, grabbing the right color, correct size panty hose in one hand. He was still trying to get Marsha Jean back on the phone to find out what she wanted.

As Jazz stood in the express lane, he saw Miss Mary. Oh yes, he had a great idea. He started motioning her to come over to the register by wildly moving his arms.

"Jazz, are you okay? Let me see what you've got in your hand," said one of the cashiers.

Just then, Miss Mary walked up.

"Buy these, change your clothes and meet me in the parking lot. I will pick you up at the door. We have got to go," Jazz whispered as quietly as possible.

Then he and Miss Mary overheard Mr. Clayton talking to the pharmacist. "No, no, no! Nothing like that. Let's just say that if you had an abrasion like a tear or your skin had been ripped similar to a rope burn. What would you recommend putting on skin to help heal an injury? I don't have all day. Please hurry," Mr. Clayton rushed.

"Jazz, did you hear that? Sounds like Mrs. Clayton is getting old and worse about falling down," Miss Mary said in a puzzled tone.

Jazz barely paid The Greeter any mind. He glanced at The Store clock and raced back to the luxury car while he continued to dial Marsha Jean's number, only to hear the busy signal still going on.

On the way to the wedding, both Miss Mary and Jazz had a good laugh about the thought of him buying panty hose.

He felt better now that Miss Mary was in the car. She could confirm his story, so no one would think he had stolen such a luxury automobile. Jazz pulled the car up in front of the mansion. One of the other parking attendants returned it to the garage.

Miss Mary took her time walking up the 13 steps of the old southern mansion. Jazz had been told that 13 was often a lucky number for some folks and the Hollingsworth based their usage of the number on the original 13 colonies. This had been passed down through the Hollingsworth family before the Civil War so that many number of steps did not make sense to Jazz.

Some folks said that there were still silver utensils buried on the grounds. If someone took the time to look, they just might find more than they bargained for out there.

The two-story white house with huge columns, giant hanging chandeliers and black shutters was a perfect accent for the enormous bricked front porch. He raced up the steps to the house as quickly as he could.

Marsha Jean welcomed him in at the door. Her hair and make-up were perfect.

"Oh, Thank God. You're back, that girl is screaming about her hose. I told her not to worry, with these big old long dresses on who would even notice. Thanks, Jazz," Marsha Jean said.

Out of breath Jazz still had one thing to say. "Marsha Jean what did you want at The Store? The phone... the phone cut off and died. I couldn't get you back..."

"Oh yeah, I was just going to tell you to hurry, but now I see I didn't have to," She said. "Oh, by the way the wedding is just about to start. I feel really bad about asking you to park cars tonight. We don't need three parking attendants. What a ridiculous idea. That was Daddy's idea and whatever Daddy wants, well... he gets. Anyway, he just came in the back door and said that since you and I had been friends for so long why don't you be my escort tonight? You know, no real southern lady goes out in public without an escort," Marsha Jean said with a wink.

He could not believe his eyes or ears.

"But... I don't have..." as usual Jazz could not talk without tripping over his own tongue.

Marsha Jean helped dignify that he did not have any suitable clothes for such a fancy occasion.

"I know it is too late for you to go all the way home and change. My brother is in town and he has a room full of clothes. You and he are about the same size. Come with me, but I'm telling you Jes-abe you are going to have to be quicker than a chunk of lard in a hot frying pan."

In the distance, music was playing softly. Someone was rushing around yelling Marsha Jean's name in the back of the house.

She motioned for him to follow her quickly up the massive staircase that looked like something from the famous movie *Gone With the Wind*. He thought he had died and gone to southern Heaven. After going down a long hall, Marsha Jean swung open two massive doors.

"You should find everything you need in here. See ya downstairs. I have to go," Marsha Jean said.

The voice yelling her name seemed to be coming closer.

Jazz went in as Marsha Jean closed the doors behind him. He could hear her dainty little feet running down the hall.

When Jazz opened the closet, it was bigger than his bedroom, bigger than the sitting room at his house. He had never seen so many fancy duds in all of his life.

He quickly chose a dark gray suit with a solid white shirt that had extra starch in the collar and in the cuffs. The tie he selected was very conservative but the shirt had a bar clamp on it which made the tie knot sit up a little around the neck.

Noticing an adjoining luxury bathroom, Jazz gave himself an S & S. This was what his mother referred to as a bath not taken in the washtub or shower because you simply did not have time. S & S stood for a body cleaning of what "smelled" and what "showed."

He used some deodorant and immediately threw on his new, borrowed clothes. He glanced in the mirror and saw that he was starting to look like a young awkward version of his daddy which pleased him greatly.

Oops... what about socks and shoes? The first dresser drawer he looked in had enough socks for the entire town to wear for a month without changing. Next, he looked everywhere for shoes, but no shoes.

As he was giving up on finding shoes, he saw a beautiful pair of lace up black leather dress shoes lying freshly shined on a velvet pillow on the bed. Jazz thought that someone must be going to wear those shoes. He laughed to himself and said: "Yeah... ME."

They were a size larger than he normally wore but they matched his suit perfectly. Feeling like a male Cinderella, he turned to exit the room. He really felt special. Jazz stopped for a moment to check himself out in the mirror. His mind churned with all kinds of thoughts and memories.

He wished his mother could see him. Another thought was just how anyone's life could change for the good or the bad in a twinkling of an eye. When he entered the room, he was Jazz the parking attendant. As he left the room, he was Sweet Jesabe, Marsha Jean's escort for the evening. What a glorious night to remember for more than one reason.

CHAPTER TWENTY-ONE

"WHEN THE ROLL is called up Yoooooooon-der! When the Roll is called up Yooooooon-der! When the Roll is called up Yooooooon-der! When the Roll is called up Yoooooon-der! I'll be there!"

Walking down that grand staircase, he recalled the last time he was dressed up. He could hear Miss Mary was singing and he remembered when she sang at his mother's funeral.

Sarah passed away early one morning. That afternoon, Miss Mary took him and Sam to The Store. Sam picked out what she wanted to wear. Jazz let Miss Mary select something for him. At the time, it did not seem to mean much to Jazz. Now looking back, he realized he was in shock. He could not believe his mother was truly gone.

They had to wait four days to bury his momma, because they were waiting on permission from Georgia Electric. When they took the farm, the company did have the decency to leave them the family cemetery. That was where Sarah wanted to be buried, right along side her kin folks. The gravesite was on a little hill under a huge water oak tree.

There was a lot of history there. Jazz's great-great-grandfather, Luther Duncan Hardee, planted that tree and named the site for the cemetery. While he, his daddy and four others carried the pine box casket up the hill, the church choir, led by Miss Mary sang, "When the Roll Is Called Up Yonder, I'll Be There!"

His mother had requested several songs, and this one was one of them. His mother's music was clearly Southern Gospel. He could still hear her singing some of her favorite songs, like "Amazing Grace," "How Great Thou Art," "In the Garden," "It Is Well With My Soul," "Victory in Jesus," "What a Friend We Have in Jesus" and, of course, "The Doxology."

As far as music went, he and his dad shared the same love for Bluegrass. The songs that came from Jazz's head sounded like part of the sound track from the movie *O Brother, Where Art Thou?*

He loved those songs and often related to the song "I Am a Man of Constant Sorrow" sung by The Soggy Bottom Boys, featuring Dan Timings. He heard those famous words play in his head and felt like it was written just for him and his dad.

Jazz and Robert often played this song at home. Just for fun, when Robert was having a good day, they locked arms and danced.

The Greeter made sure Jazz's world had been filled with music — mostly music traditional in the back Georgia woods, like Bluegrass and Southern Gospel. However, Miss Mary did take a shine to some easy listening tunes, as well as some classical music. No high brow melodies for Jazz though.

Robert occasionally listened to country music when Sarah was not around. She never took too kindly to that sort of music. She said country songs told stories of woe and discontent, usually about somebody's heart being broken over cheating.

Sarah thought she already had too many problems of her own to be worried about and did not want to add the sorrows folks had in them country songs to her already long list of troubles.

Jazz took pride in having heard so many Christian and Bluegrass groups sing at his church, including the famous Byrd Family. Their God-given talents left him mesmerized. He also relished hearing Sheriff Rowe sing. His favorite song the sheriff sang was "Swing Down Sweet Chariot."

Jazz left the Hollingsworth mansion and went into the backyard. There was a long back porch with several steps leading down to the wedding area then another set of 13 steps.

He felt as if he were walking into a magnificent picture postcard. The grounds were recently mowed and countless fresh-cut floral arrangements were everywhere.

There was a permanent rose garden to the left side of where the wedding congregation was sitting. Jazz believed the aroma of fresh flowers was relaxing and must be what heaven smelled like.

There were at least 300 chairs with at least 450 people. The ceremony area was the most wonderful, newly painted gazebo — heavily decorated with various colors of roses. The view was even more magnificent, looking out over the Hollingsworth Lake that fed into the Manicar River. Two white swans were gliding around the lake on opposite ends from each other.

A string quartet and a piano were softly playing some classical song Jazz did not recognize. Needless to say the music was not his style.

The wedding party began to exit from the back door of the house. First came Dr. Cummings with Conner, the ring bearer, and Matilda, the flower girl. Conner was wearing a cute little, black tuxedo with tails and Matilda was wearing a long, white lace dress with a circle of flowers headpiece sitting on her beautiful, long blonde curly hair. She was carrying a gorgeous basket of flower pedals.

Dr. Cummings was wearing a dress that matched Matilda's. She was beautiful, too. Everyone immediately began to ooh and ahh as the three of them walked down the steps. It was a Kodak moment indeed. Cameras started flashing.

Miss Mary got up and sang "Whither Thou

Goest I Will Go" accompanied by the ebony grand piano.

The wedding party continued down the steps as Miss Mary's melodious voice filled the countryside, and she looked grand. Even though Miss Mary had less than an hour to prepare, she still looked better than most folks who had been getting ready all day to be there. Miss Mary was wearing a long, light blue formal gown with white, high-heeled shoes to match.

Jazz quickly thought about The Store. No matter what the occasion, The Store had whatever you needed.

A few bridesmaids and their attendants came out next. Then, an angel appeared by herself. Her long, beautiful, golden hair appeared ready for a movie close-up. The southern belle gown looked perfect. Marsha Jean was her sister's maid of honor. Jazz was so taken by her beauty, he forgot to breath.

As the rest of the wedding party descended the stairs, Miss Mary's song came to a crescendo, and smoothly ended. She hastily sat down, up close to the front, just as Miss Vera began to recite a poem that she wrote for this momentous occasion.

As Miss Mary moved to her seat, she motioned for Jazz to sit with her. He was relieved he did not have to stand up any longer. His feet were starting to hurt. Even though the shoes were bigger than his usual size, the pair made for a narrow fit on Jazz's wide foot.

The music continued with a soft, string version of "Here Comes the Bride." Everyone was almost in place at the back of the sitting area. Matilda followed instructions and gently threw flower petals on the ground while she walked down the center aisle. When she knew someone she would stop and go over to them to give the guest a flower. People were pointing and giggling at her two-year-old actions. Conner was doing great, until he saw the lake.

"Momma look! Can I go fishing a little bit?"

Everyone laughed so hard they did not really notice the attendants had all marched in and were in their designated place in front of the gazebo. As soon as everyone was ready, the Reverend Bentley, the groom and the groom's best man walked out from the side of the house.

"Will everyone please stand?" Boomed what seemed like the voice of God.

The First Baptist Church preacher was attending a convention out of town. It did not seem to matter much to the Hollingsworth family. The Reverend Bentley was a well liked and very well respected man in the community.

When the ceremony ended, the two white swans had come together and were gracefully paddling side by side. A few folks gave out a sigh of awe and some even shed tears of joy. Jazz thought it was quite a beautiful scene.

He and Miss Mary talked about all of this

later. The Greeter told him she believed the swans were symbolic of the union between a husband and wife. He had not thought of it, but he always knew Miss Mary had a way of making most anything have deep meaning.

As the wedding couple turned to leave the gazebo for the reception, the preacher introduced the couple and the band began to play one of Jazz's favorite songs. Mama Sugar and The Hallelujah Voices belted out their own jazzy version of "Oh Happy Day!"

This festive mood didn't last long.

CHAPTER TWENTY-TWO

MISS VERA'S CAKE was by far the biggest, grandest confectionary sweet Jazz had ever seen. From the comments at the reception, everybody in town thought so, too. Folks stood next to the cake to have pictures taken. Marsha Jean was the ultimate social butterfly and talked to everyone. Miss Mary was her natural self, too, as she greeted folks.

Even if no one else noticed, Miss Mary made a big deal out of how Jazz was dressed.

"My, my, you're looking handsome today. You're growing up, Jazz. I know your mama would be so proud of you," Miss Mary went on.

Jazz was grateful she did not ask where the clothes or shoes came from. Right then he longed to go and put his old sneakers on.

She patted him on the back, as if she was pleased with him. "Come on Jazz. Let's go get something to eat before it's all gone," Miss Mary said, with a laugh.

It sounded good to Jazz. He often forgot to eat, unless he was reminded or everyone else was eating something, too. Still, he knew it would be a long time before all this food was gone.

DJ Mr. Mix from a local radio station was starting to play some upbeat popular music, along with a mixture of requests. He was a local celebrity and Jazz was thrilled to finally see the sharp dressed Mr. Mix in person. His real name was Clarence Mixon, but everyone called him Mr. Mix.

As Miss Mary and Jazz started down one of the food tables, Miss Mary pulled out a check made out to the "Matthew Lumpkin Transplant Fund" for five thousand dollars. Jazz's eyes bugged out of his head! She quickly put it back in her pocket.

Jazz was speechless.

Miss Mary continued to put food on her tray as if it was a daily occurrence for the fund to receive such a large amount of a donation.

"Mr. Jonah C. Cauldwell is the chief executive officer and president of the legal business the Hollingsworths and the groom work for. He and his wife, Sandy, flew in from Virginia last night on their private jet, rented a limousine, drove up from Augusta and spent the night here at the mansion. We had a snappy, yet very friendly chat last night when I delivered the groom's hummingbird cake and I practiced the songs I sang tonight.

"I asked him did he think he could help us folks out in this little town. He said he thought so but he wanted to discuss it with Sandy. I heard both of them are very smart; they make decisions together. So today, right before the wedding, he handed this to me. There you have it. What a great guy. This is almost what we have raised so far," Miss Mary said. "And remember about the Wal-Mart commitment?"

Jazz shook his head, as he was being forced down the magnificent display of food. He had never, ever seen so much free food in one place in his life. This put him into deep thought, until Miss Mary finally broke through.

"The Store is going to match whatever we can raise. So today we technically raised $10,000 for Matthew's transplant! Praise God and Glory Be," Miss Mary whispered.

Jazz stopped dead in his tracks in shock. However, the line pushed him on in a minute.

When they got to the end of the line, Miss Mary's plate was full. Jazz's plate, unfortunately, had only a square of cheddar cheese on it. He had stopped putting food on his plate when he heard the unbelievable news about the large donation.

Jazz and Miss Mary headed to find two seats next to Marsha Jean. As they approached her table, she waved at them to come on over.

"Hey Jes-abe, you look great," she said.

Jazz wanted to say something nice back to Marsha Jean but he just knew it would come out wrong. "Thanks. You boo," was what he said.

He meant "you, too."

Fortunately, the music was so loud she did not notice. Clowns walked around doing tricks and blowing up balloons for the children.

Dr. Cummings took Conner down to the lake so he could go "fishing a little bit," as promised. The Hollingsworths did not mind, and even provided a fishing pole.

Matilda threw bread into the water to feed the fish, the ducks and the swans. Her beautiful, curly, strawberry blond hair was shining brilliantly in the glow of the setting sun.

Jazz looked around and thought he saw everyone in town at the reception. Mr. Thigpen was not wearing his usual coveralls, rather a handsome dark blue suit. Mrs. Turnbow was sporting a large exquisite, off-white lace hat with matching dress, shoes and of course, gloves that buttoned on the inside. During all of her conversations, Mrs. Turnbow waved her arms to show off her gloves.

Jazz truly knew it was a formal occasion, once he saw the long length of her white gloves.

"These are my long, off white formal ones. The Colonel, God rest his soul, gave these to me on the morning of my wedding day. Yes, a most eventful time in my life!" She reminded Jazz of what an older angel must look like.

Jazz and Miss Mary sat down with Marsha Jean and a few other employees from The Store, including Mr. Roberto.

"Oh Miss Mary, by the way, your graduation party idea really helped out the lawn and garden department. I was showing the sales figures to Mr. Johnston and he was quite impressed. He said it might even become a tradition," Mr. Roberto said with pride.

"Great. Would anyone like something to drink? I'm going to get some punch. All that singing made me thirsty," Miss Mary declared, promptly changing the subject.

"Give this to the bride!" a loud voice came from nowhere as someone shoved Miss Mary hard in the back. Miss Mary turned as Mr. Clayton practically punched a hole in her back with the corner of a large, wrapped package. As soon as she took it, Mr. Clayton stomped away. Miss Mary started after him.

"Charles... wait... stop," Miss Mary yelled over the music as she followed Mr. Clayton and motioned for Jazz to come along as well. Jazz followed.

"Charles... please... How is Diana? I am so worried about her. And, today in The Store, you did not even speak."

Mr. Clayton stopped, but did not turn around. By now, Miss Mary and Jazz had caught up. They stood directly in front of him. Sugar Pie did not want to look either one of them in the face.

"What has happened to her? Did the pharmacist give you any medicine for her skin?" Miss Mary continued with sincere compassion.

Mr. Clayton looked surprised she had

overheard his conversation. "Don't be worried about her," he snapped back. "She is fine, just old age catching up with that ancient bat."

Jazz was flabbergasted.

"Charles, Diana's been falling a lot lately and I haven't seen her in The Store," Miss Mary said looking bewildered. "Is there anything we can do? I went by your house to visit, but no one answered the door."

Miss Mary laid her hand on Mr. Clayton's arm, but only momentarily.

"You best not be coming to my house. You hear me? Everybody's always saying you are a nosy ole gossip. Well, they're right," Mr. Clayton retorted. He pushed her hand off his arm as he crushed her heart. This time he left without anyone stopping him.

Jazz and Miss Mary stood in a moment of silence, watching as Mr. Clayton left.

"Don't worry about him, Miss Mary. You know people start acting funny when they get old," Jazz said, as he repeated what he had heard.

"I'm fine. I'm fine," declared Miss Mary as if saying this twice would make it so.

"Something's wrong, Jazz. You mark my words. Something is wrong!" Miss Mary had a look of deep concern on her face.

In the background, Mr. Mix was playing a love song for the couple's first, slow dance — Shania Twain's "From This Moment."

CHAPTER TWENTY-THREE

IT WAS DARK NOW, but Mrs. Hollingsworth made sure the back yard was lit up with tiny strings of white lights.

Jazz remembered when she came in The Store and bought three carts full of nothing but lights. This was right after Christmas. Now, he knew why. Jazz thought it looked magical as he happily recalled what Six Flags looked like at night.

The whole wedding and reception was like a dream come true. Suddenly all the lights went out — surely the Hollingsworth's had paid their light bill.

Flashes of brilliant colored lights illuminated the sky with the most magnificent flares. Standing next to Marsha Jean, he watched the fireworks explode over Hollingsworth Lake. Jazz had never even heard of fireworks at a wedding.

Afterwards, the couple opened their gifts. The last present was an envelope with keys to a set of matching cars from her parents, his and her brand new BMW M3s — just like Mr. Hollingsworth's car, except dark metallic blue. The license plates were ALP 1 and ALP 2. The letters stood for Assurance Legal Plans.

Jazz smiled — he knew what it felt like to drive a BMW M3.

The bride and groom left in a six-horse drawn carriage that looked like a fairy tale. It reminded Jazz of Cinderella going to the ball. Some yelled out: "Where'd the fancy ride come from?"

"Daddy knows somebody and worked it all out," Marsha Jean said with a grin. "Had it shipped up from Florida, but it has to be back no later than Tuesday by midnight. I told daddy if he didn't have it back on time he might be turned into an ugly rat!"

Everyone laughed.

As the newlyweds left, several hundred doves were released, and three of the string players in the orchestra played "Somewhere in Time."

Mr. Hollingsworth thanked everyone for coming and let the guests know the couple would ride to the end of the drive, where a SUV limousine would get them and take the blissful duo to the Augusta Regional Airport.

The honeymoon would consist of flying from Augusta to Atlanta to stay at the Hyatt Regency overnight. The next day, the couple would fly to New York for several Broadway shows and to see the sites for a few days. After that, the couple would go to Europe, where they planned on spending a month.

Jazz just knew this wedding would make the front page of The Evanston Times — maybe even a whole edition would be devoted to it.

Some people milled around after the bride and groom had made their grand exit. Most folks had started their journey home with comments like, "I've never seen anything like this in my life!" As a souvenir, the guests were given a porcelain statue of two doves kissing. The gold inscription had the couple's names and their wedding date on the side.

Most certainly, the Woods had never before seen any event like this one. Jazz was truly glad he had been there.

Jazz, Miss Mary and Marsha Jean told everyone good-bye.

"Hey I don't know about ya'll, but I am so hungry I could eat a horse," Marsha Jean confessed to Miss Mary and Jazz. "Well, maybe not that much, but I sure could eat a lot! I'm sure there is plenty of food left. Let's go have something to eat and drink. I'm mighty thirsty, too."

Jazz and Miss Mary agreed. The staff was putting away food and cleaning up the grounds. Marsha Jean managed to stop them in time for her and her two compadres to eat to the point of being overly satisfied.

The DJ and the orchestra were packing up to leave. The rain that drenched the town earlier in the week was gone. The hot, summer sun had dried up all the puddles. The night was clear and the stars were out. The peaceful songs of the crickets around the lake were now dominant and could be heard throughout The Woods, a most familiar, relaxing summer sound at night in the South.

Miss Mary, Marsha Jean and Jazz sat in the gazebo softly talking.

The two young folks had long since changed back into what they called their play clothes. They laughed and recalled how their mother's would tell them to take off their Sunday clothes and go put their play clothes as soon as they came back from church.

Both were wearing some of the most popular Faded Glory styles. Marsha Jean's clothes were new — just arrived on the Tuesday shipment this past week. Jazz's were more like two years ago, but still looked good.

The Store bound them together in different ways. Tonight the three talked about various things, mostly the wedding.

Miss Mary commented on how all of the attendants were wearing a gold charm bracelet with a picture of the bride and groom etched on it. Marsha Jean explained these were presents from her sister and it was something that could be ordered at the Wal-Mart jewelry department.

She was very excited about offering pictures on charms as well as special occasion items.

She had ordered her school ring from there. Marsha Jean proudly showed off her graduation symbol to Jazz and Miss Mary. They both thought it was quite nice.

Jazz felt at ease and very comfortable with his friends, so he decided to discuss something very special with them. He was surprised at how at home he felt.

"I want to share something with you... both of you," he said deliberately.

They both silently nodded their heads.

"At the graduation party at The Store, Sam gave me an envelope," he explained, as he slowly reached into his back pocket and dragged it out of a well worn leather billfold.

"Inside the envelope was a fifty-dollar Wal-Mart gift certificate; the card said from "Your Wal-Mart Family, Sam & Dad." I know this was from both of you as well as Miss Vera and Mr. Roberto. So, I wanted to tell you thank you. This really means a great deal to me. As we all know..."

They all chimed in simultaneously, "A Wal-Mart gift certificate comes in everybody's perfect size and color."

This was what Mr. Johnston had drilled in their heads over and over. They all laughed, especially Marsha Jean. Jazz figured she had never heard him really say anything funny before. They acknowledged his gratefulness quickly because they could sense that he had something else to say.

"Also, in the envelope was this," Jazz said. He handed the ladies an old picture of a young couple, a little boy and a little baby. The woman was cradling the baby in her arms. Jazz thought Miss Mary recognized the family from long ago because a pleasant smile crept across her face. Marsha Jean had a puzzled expression, apparently because she did not know who it was.

"There was a letter, too," he said.

Jazz handed the letter to Miss Mary. Even though it was dark out, the light of the full moon would enable her to see it.

"You want me to read this out loud Jazz?" Miss Mary asked.

He bobbed his head like a fake dog on the car dashboard. She reached into her skirt pocket and pulled out her glasses.

"My dearest most darling son, Jesabe," Miss Mary said and then paused. Sarah had written Jazz a letter before she died. Marsha Jean put a hand over her mouth.

"I am writing this letter to you knowing that I will not be there in person for you on the most important days of your life, but I will be there for you in spirit. I asked your father to give this to you when you graduate from high school along with a picture of the family.

"This picture was taken the day we brought Sammy Jo home from the hospital. I don't know if I ever told you this, but I had Sam for you. I wanted you to have a friend and someone you could always play with, count on. Just give her the opportunity — she will be there for you.

"I am not sure if I ever actually told you, but Sam named you Jazz. She couldn't pronounce Jesabe at first, so everyone knows you as Jazz now because of her. She always looked up to you and admired you. Be good to her.

"Your daddy is a good, kind, strong man. You can depend on him for many years to come. We might not have always understood some of his ways, but he loved all of us just the same."

Sarah was spared the horror of knowing Robert had lung cancer when she passed away. He was ill while she was dying, but he kept the illness to himself until it was too late, then Jazz and Sam as well as everyone else in The Woods noticed. Perhaps if he had gone on to the doctor earlier — Robert might have been cured.

Miss Mary continued to read Sarah's letter. "I'm glad all of you have Miss Mary..." Miss Mary stopped to choke back tears. "She has been a pillar of strength and kindness over the years. We are blessed to have her. People love you, Jazz. Trust in them and they will be there for you. Always remember I love you, I loved you even before you were born.

"I prayed for a special little baby we could love and give a special name, too. I wanted your name to be different, yet full of history and meaning so your daddy and I came up with Jesabe Washington. Never forget you are named after our precious savior, Jesus as well as the great President Abe Lincoln and together this makes Jesabe. Two fine role models for you son. Your middle name, Washington, was after the road in town that can lead you anywhere in the world, but can always bring you back home to The Woods. The road was named after the first president, George Washington when he came through here on his way to Augusta.

"I have very little, but I am leaving you and Sammy Jo mama's Bible. You know how much I loved your grandma. This book is more precious than silver or gold. As far as religion and all, I believe the Bible is true and holy. 'Look up into the hills from which cometh thy strength.'

"Cumberland Woods was my home. It always gave me hope and courage. I know money has been scarce, but we did the best we could. Having nothing at least teaches you to depend on yourself, your family, your friends, your country and above all God.

"Your daddy and I prayed over you the night that you were born with a prayer cloth that was anointed with olive oil from Jerusalem. It's yours now," Miss Mary read with emotion.

Jazz gently pulled it out of his plaid, short sleeved cotton shirt pocket and showed it to his best friends in the world. Then, he put it back and buried his face into his hands. As if the weight of the world fell on his shoulders, Jazz felt a sense of hopelessness.

"Robert prayed you would have good morals. His prayers were answered. You do us proud. Fight the good fight. Remember me, and keep your eyes on the cross so that when the roll is called up yonder, you'll be there. Look up to the heavens and know I'm waiting for you. I love you.

With love from the bottom of my heart, Your Mama, Sarah."

Miss Mary felt a lump in her throat as the tears began to well up in her eyes. Marsha Jean wept silently as she laid her hand on Jazz's back. Both ladies wiped the tears streaming down their faces. Miss Mary moved closer to Jazz and laid her hand on his back.

In silence, the old woman and young girl took Jazz by the hands and walked to the edge of the moonlit water in Marsha Jean's back yard. Looking up, the peace and awesome presence of Sarah was felt.

The loss of his mother a year earlier combined with the uncertainty of what would happen when his father died was almost too much to bear. Yet, somehow he was in awe of the overwhelming vastness of the universe as he looked up into the heavens.

CHAPTER TWENTY-FOUR

EVEN THOUGH IT WAS a Saturday in July, almost every day seemed like Saturday because summer had arrived. People needed Jazz more than ever to retrieve shopping carts. Miss Mary was always so encouraging. "Jazz you do such a great job," she said.

He got a full-time position after graduation and was able to work more hours.

Independence Day brought everyone to town — people needed all kinds of supplies and food to make the holiday special.

He remembered before The Store opened. When party goers ran out of something — like charcoal or potato salad — they just went without.

"Well... hello Stan," Miss Mary exclaimed. "I haven't seen you in a month of Sundays! How have you been?" Stan Horton was the bank president. She was teasing him because he came in The Store at least once a day, some days two and three times.

As Mr. Horton began to reply, he pulled out a meticulously pressed white men's handkerchief with blue embroidered initials in one corner and wiped perspiration from his brow.

"I have been just fine. Just Fine. Finer than frog hair," he said with a laugh.

At that moment, Conner, Matilda and Dr. Cummings entered The Store. As usual nothing got past Conner.

"Mr. Horton from the bank, Mommy look," said Conner as he tugged his mother's freshly pressed pink cotton shirt.

"Okay Conner, I see," Dr. Cummings said. "Hi Miss Mary, Mr. Horton. How are you both doing today?"

"Mr. Horton, I hate to be the one to tell you, but frogs don't have hair," Conner corrected the bank president. "I know — I pick them up and squeeze them like this all the time." Conner began demonstrating his treatment of frogs by squeezing an imaginary one. Everyone laughed.

"Toys," Conner blurted. "Can we go look at the toys?"

As Dr. Cummings picked up Matilda and Conner to place them in a shopping cart for two children, she turned to Miss Mary.

"I believe there are certain sayings that all children must have in common, such as 'Are we there yet?' the entire duration of a trip," Dr. Cummings continued her observation. "Then, when you arrive at The Store, they want to know

'Can we go look at the toys?' Seems as if no matter how much bargaining with them, like 'When we get to The Store, I need to do some shopping and if you are good we will look at the toys does not seem to work."

Both women nodded and smiled.

Suddenly, "God Bless America" began to play on Mr. Horton's cellular phone. He stepped to the side while The Greeter did what she did best, greeted.

Jazz and Miss Mary heard the banker's conversation. The cart pusher thought the connection must have been bad because Mr. Horton was speaking a little louder than usual.

"No... oh, NO. I explained all of that to him last week," Mr. Horton said, raising his tone. "She must be with him if he is going to withdraw all of his money because on the account, it specifically states both of their names. No, I don't know why he wants to withdraw everything...Yes, Yes... I know it's quite a large sum of money they have accumulated over the years. He made several excellent investment choices... But he is going to have to bring her in so she can sign the proper paperwork — for that amount of money there's a three day waiting period."

Mr. Horton was silent for a moment while he listened to the person on the other end of the line talk. "No... I went through all of that! All I can say is he is getting old and... I know... I know... perhaps he came in and you just reminded him.... Oh... so he acted like he did not know all that... but still wanted the cash now? Well... I'm over at Wal-Mart... I just had to get some... Okay... Listen to me, go back out front and tell him I am on my way. I'll walk back over there in just a minute. Thanks."

The bank was so close — it was practically in the Wal-Mart parking lot.

"Stan, The Store is this way," Miss Mary said jokingly as Mr. Horton turned to leave. She pointed inside with a big grin on her face.

"Oh... well... something has come up and I have to get back to the bank right away. See ya later," Mr. Horton said quickly.

Between customers Jazz spoke quietly, but there was anxiety in his young voice. "Miss Mary, did you hear that?"

Miss Mary nodded her head. "Mr. Horton had to have been talking about Mr. Clayton," she whispered. "Something's wrong at the Clayton house, I just know it!"

"Something's wrong at the Clayton house?" Jazz repeated her words with uncertainty. "Do you think something has happened to Mrs. Clayton? Surely not! I mean this doesn't sound good at all. Come to think of it... we certainly haven't seen her in The Store in a while. Now, Mr. Clayton wants to withdraw all of his money. What do you think?"

"I don't know Jazz, but I'm working on it," Miss Mary said.

Dr. Cummings wheeled her cart back to the front. "Where're the batteries? The children's toys are constantly in need of those tiny power supplies."

Miss Mary smiled and offered the location, while suggesting the ones that were on sale. Dr. Cummings thanked her and continued on her way as the children waved and blew kisses to their Me-Me.

"Don't have time to talk," Mr. Thigpen said as he walked in the door. "Where are the batteries? Having a family Fourth of July gathering and we need the music outside so where are the batteries?"

Mr. Thigpen didn't slow down long enough to hear the answer, but Miss Mary gave a brief one anyway. She gave directions according to what people were interested in. Mr. Thigpen knew where the sporting goods department was, so she started by giving directions from that area.

There seemed to be a real need for batteries this time of year, but when Jazz thought about it, batteries were needed all the time.

As Jazz slow-poked back outside, he instantly noticed the weather was hot and sticky, the air hot and dusty. The humidity was so high, he felt like someone was using a hair dryer on his whole body.

Everyone had the air conditioning on in their cars — partly to avoid getting dust in the cars. Jazz thought it was kind of odd the

Clayton's rode around with their windows down. "No matter how dusty these old country Georgia roads are in The Woods, I still like the smell of fresh air — even if it's hot air," Mrs. Clayton would say. Of course, that was before she stopped coming in The Store.

There were volunteers at The Store raising money for the Back to School Supplies promotion for folks who couldn't afford to purchase these item. Jazz thought it was a great idea. The program helped his family out several times. No one at school knew it though — which was the best part to him.

"Hey, Jazz. What time do you get off?" Miss Mary asked between customers.

Jazz just knew they would go pay the Claytons a visit.

"Four o'clock this afternoon," he answered. "What were you thinking about?"

"Well... I was thinking about going to visit some sick folks in the hospital. I just thought I would like some company. That is if you don't have any other plans," Miss Mary said, as if she was analyzing the overall situation

"No, I want to go... just wasn't what I was expecting," he said.

Then again, things never did seem to turn out the way Jazz was expecting them to.

CHAPTER TWENTY-FIVE

THE RIDE INTO AUGUSTA was a pleasant one. Usually, Miss Mary seemed compelled to keep at least a minimum discussion going, but this evening silence seemed to dominate the trip.

Jazz's head spun with ideas and thoughts pertaining to Mrs. Clayton's safety. He was forced to speak just before they arrived at the hospital.

"Miss Mary... I was wondering ..." he started. "Why are we here at the MCG Hospital in Augusta? I just really feel like we need to go see about Mrs. Clayton," Jazz blurted out.

Silence returned, for what seemed like an eternity. As Miss Mary turned the wheels to the left from Fifteenth Street to drive into the hospital parking deck, she reached over as a loving mother would and patted Jazz's left shoulder.

"You've gotta trust me," Miss Mary said.

He did.

After the car was parked, they got out and walked into the hospital lobby. She went over to the information booth and Jazz followed.

"Good Evening! What room is Matthew Lumpkin in? I understand he has been moved from the Children's Center across the street," Miss Mary inquired politely.

"Yes, he is here in the CCU, coronary care unit. He's 18 now, you know," the young receptionist with long, flowing black hair replied with a friendly smile.

She slowly turned and flung her hair to her back so she could see the clock on the wall behind her.

"If you hurry you can make visitation," she said. "Every so many hours the family and friends can visit him for 15 minutes. Everyone here at the hospital is really rooting for Matthew. Are you folks from his home town?"

Miss Mary and Jazz nodded.

"I know folks over in Evanston must really miss him and his family," she said. "The Lumpkins are real jewels."

Jazz really liked the beautiful, young lady, but he felt he was betraying Marsha Jean, so he tried not to look at her. To him, she looked like the actress Angelina Jolie.

"Ya'll stop back by and see me on your way out. I'll be here till 9 o'clock. I'd like to know how Matthew is doing. I haven't had a chance to check on him today," the young girl explained.

After they took the elevator up and trotted down the hall, Jazz and Miss Mary caught sight of Matthew's parents straightaway. His mother was crying softly.

"Ruth... Joseph," Miss Mary called their names. Everyone in The Woods had heard Matthew's time was running short, unless a donor was found very soon. He had already out lived the doctors' expectations.

"Hi Miss Mary, Jazz. Looks like Matthew made another turn for the worse. His white blood count dropped severely," Mr. Lumpkin offered the latest information.

"We don't want to bother you, but we did want to see if there was anything that we can do. Your family is in our thoughts and prayers. Also, we wanted you to know we have been able to raise $19,600 for Matthew's transplant," Miss Mary shared with pride.

Everyone knew this was not enough money, but Miss Mary wanted to share some great news with the Lumpkins in hopes of making them feel better.

Mrs. Lumpkin wept and made her way to Miss Mary's loving arms.

"Thank you so very much! Thank you. I just hope we get a chance to use that money," Matthew's mother said through her tears. She had cried so much, her face was swollen.

Suddenly, the double doors swung open and a nurse came out to make the evening announcement. "Any visitors to see the patients must come with me now. This will be the last visitation for the day. No one can stay longer than 15 minutes. Thank you for your cooperation," the nurse babbled, all in one breath.

One by one, people who had been sitting for most of the day in what looked like the most uncomfortable chairs peeled themselves out and stood up. They looked like they had been through this drill many times.

"Do you want to see him again or would you like Miss Mary and Jazz to visit this time?" Mr. Lumpkin lovingly asked his wife, who was still crying.

"No, please, you both go this time," Mrs. Lumpkin said. "I want him to know other people really do care enough about him to come all the way over from The Woods to see him."

Miss Mary and Jazz immediately followed the nurse. The doors were starting to close so they rushed to get inside. Once the nurse found out who they were visiting, she asked them to put on hospital robes and masks before entering Matthew's room.

In the room, Jazz gasped at all of the equipment and the sounds coming from them — as well as from Matthew. Each breath Matthew made was a struggle.

Jazz looked at him and almost did not recognize his friend. The Woods' visitors stood and stared at the young man for a few minutes; it looked like he was asleep.

No matter what ailed somebody, Jazz

thought, the illness seemed to rob people of their dignity and appearance as well as their names. This did not look like the same young man who went to school with Jazz. This was not the same young man who constantly played practical jokes on everyone.

Jazz remembered the time Matthew put a frog in Marsha Jean's lunch box when they were in the fourth grade. Her scream could have been heard in three counties. There were several memories of good times these two boys shared. They had grown-up together, but their lives had taken different roads.

Matthew opened his eyes and gave a slight smile. With much effort, he raised his right hand to show that he was glad to see them. Jazz knew Matthew did not have enough energy to talk.

Miss Mary had no trouble finding words. She could make anything sound exciting.

"Hey Matthew, it's me and Jazz here underneath these masks. I can't wait to see you get up and come back to The Woods. Everyone misses you. I thought about you today. Yes, I did. We had volunteers over at The Store taking up donations for our Back to School Supplies promotion to help folks out. I knew you would have been there if you could. Also, I wanted you to know that your pet fish, Mr. Fried is doing just fine. I still think you naming a fish Fried is hilarious... Fried Fish! Don't worry about him — I won't let anyone eat him."

Everyone smiled. Matthew raised his hand and gave a deliberate thumbs up.

"Jazz, you want to tell Matthew something," Miss Mary said in a telling, not asking tone.

"Well... Matt," Jazz smiled as he cautiously chose his words. "We've had some great times together. Remember that time you ..."

"Visitation time for the CCU is over. You must leave now. You may come back tomorrow starting at 10 a.m. Thank you!"

The nurse's announcement seemed to come out of nowhere like an alarm to evacuate the unit of intruders, more commonly known as visitors.

"What Jazz is trying to say is that the two of you have had some great times, and I am sure there are a lot more to come," Miss Mary said. "We love you and are praying for you. We'll see you again soon."

They waved before hurrying out the door.

As they left the CCU, the Lumpkins exchanged hugs and kisses with Miss Mary. Jazz shook Mr. Lumpkin's hand. They all meandered down the hall and stepped on the elevator together. Mr. Lumpkin pressed the button for the first floor. As the elevator doors opened, the Lumpkin's got off.

Jazz started to step off, when Miss Mary held one hand out in front of him and the other reached over to push the button to close the door. Brief goodbyes were exchanged. He leaned over slightly to one side so he was able to catch a glimpse of the beautiful girl at the information desk as the doors closed. Jazz looked confused and wondered where they were going as the elevator started back up.

CHAPTER TWENTY-SIX

MISS MARY KNOCKED on a patient's door and Jazz learned they were visiting their beloved Medicine Man, Doc.

News still traveled at a snail's pace in The Woods, so it was nearly two days before Jazz found out Doc was still alive after his fall. He hadn't seen Doc since and kept picturing him on the floor of The Store back in April.

Standing outside his hospital door, they heard Doc snoring. Jazz thought this was a good sign, a great sign in fact. Even if somebody snoring got on your nerves at least it showed they were still alive and kicking. That was a good thing.

Miss Mary began to slowly push open the door. "Knock, knock. Guess who?"

The old man sat in bed, wearing the traditional, unflattering hospital gown. However, he always did have a touch of class about him. On top of the gown was a gorgeous, plush burgundy robe with his initials -- WHB -- embroidered in gold on the front top pocket.

Doc was sitting in a chair next to a window that looked out over the parking deck. Jazz thought it was really awesome to be so high off of the ground, the tenth floor! The lights of the big city twinkled in Jazz's eyes. Doc graciously stood to his feet as if the great commander had arrived.

"Well," he began. "Mary and Jazz, aren't you both a sight for sore eyes, huh?"

This was the only real grandfather figure Jazz had ever known. Doc and Miss Mary both had presents for his and Sam's birthday as well as Christmas each year for as long as Jazz could remember, since they left the farm. They both hugged Doc and loved him for different reasons.

"Sit down. Sit Down," Doc told his visitors. "Tell this old country doctor what's going on in his neck of The Woods, huh?"

Miss Mary and Doc took turns flap-jawing. She bragged on Jazz for graduating from high school and his perfect attendance certificate.

"Jazz, here got 100 percent attendance from kindergarten through the twelfth grade! Imagine that?" Mary proclaimed.

Jazz listened and smiled for awhile, but did not really join in the conversation. He felt like they wanted to talk just between the two of them, so he told them he was going to stretch his legs a minute. He excused himself and made a mad dash for the elevator. The clock on the wall indicated that it was 8:45 p.m.

He was trying to make it back to the information desk to see if the young woman was still there. His plan was not to talk to her, but to walk by and perhaps she might say something to him.

Blocking the elevator doors was someone mopping. The little yellow caution signs were set out to warn people to be careful and not to fall. Thanks to Mr. Roberto, Jazz recognized the Spanish word for caution on the sign, cuidado.

"Watch your step," the man said as he moved the mop wildly from side to side. Jazz gave up on trying to even reach the elevator button. It was 8:50 p.m. He had to hurry. As he spotted the sign to the stairs, he ran and pushed open the door. Ten flights of stairs in 10 minutes. He could do it.

"Visiting hours will be over in 10 minutes, please begin to gather up your belongings in order to leave. Visiting hours begin again in the morning at 9 a.m. Thank you," the intercom announced.

Jazz noticed visiting hours for the CCU and regular hospital patients were different. He figured folks like Matthew needed more rest than others.

By the time he made the last step, he was completely out of breath. As soon as he pushed open the exit door into the hospital lobby, he could see that the girl was gone and there was a sign on the counter. As he got closer, he could read the message: "Will be back at 9 a.m."

He went back up to Doc's room by way of the elevator. As he exited, Miss Mary and Doc's laughter could be heard down the hall. The sound was pleasant and refreshing to Jazz.

"I know it's time to go, but we just got here," Miss Mary said in a disappointed tone.

At that moment, they turned to see Jazz coming in. Both the elderly man and woman's eyes glowed with delight as if he were their son.

"Jazz, I appreciate you going over and checking on things while I'm away," Doc said. "I owe you! When I get back on my feet, I'll be settling up with you, huh?"

The doctor took solace in knowing he would eventually leave the hospital — at least one more time.

"Andy... or rather I should say Dr. Howard, comes to see me almost every morning while he is doing his rounds," Doc said. "Guess he will be taking over for me before too long. He saved my life, because if he hadn't of been there to give me CPR when he did... well, I might just be having to talk to you good folks right now through a long, very long distance call from heaven, huh?"

They all chuckled. Then, Miss Mary reached inside a blue Wal-Mart plastic bag she had been toting and pulled out a paper plate covered with aluminum foil.

A big, grin crept across Doc's face.

"Now, how'd you know that there's nothing better that you could've brought me than a slice of your hummingbird cake, huh? I can see it now, when you become famous you'll be marketing these cakes and each one will have a disclaimer that states: "No hummingbirds were injured while preparing this cake," Doc humorously added.

A hearty, clean laugh filled the room for a moment. The goodbyes were exchanged. Doc noticed and commented Miss Mary was still wearing the hummingbird pin that he had given her two years ago for Christmas. She smiled.

While Jazz pushed on the heavy, polished wooden door to leave, Miss Mary turned to Doc, "Oh, by the way..."

She was interrupted by the intercom announcement. "Visiting hours are now over. Please exit the hospital at this time."

"What do you know about Johnny Clayton?" Miss Mary finished, determined to ask before they left.

A look of horror came over Doc's face, a look that Jazz had never seen before on him. He leaped out of his chair as if it were on fire.

"You don't have time to hear what I know about Johnny Clayton! That boy was nothing but trouble since the day they adopted him," Doc said in an irate tone, squinting his eyes. "His parents were killed in a car accident when he was a little boy. His biological mother and Diana were sisters. I wouldn't be surprised if he didn't do it!

Most people in The Woods don't know what terror he put Charles and Diana through…"

Miss Mary and Jazz were spellbound. A nurse entered the room to take Doc's vital signs.

"Ma'am, sir, it's time for you to leave. The patient needs to rest," she said to Miss Mary and Jazz.

"Oh hush ya belly aching… you can come back in a minute," Doc admonished the nurse. "These are my people from my hometown over in Cumberland Woods. Ya'll come on and I'll walk you to the elevator. Will that satisfy ya, huh?"

He was used to being in charge and not having anyone tell him what to do.

"Sir, visitation hours are over. You really don't need any more exercise today. A man in your condition…" the nurse said.

She could be heard as the three of them joined arm in arm going down the hall. Jazz thought they looked like a scene from The *Wizard of Oz*. They were almost in a huddle anxiously waiting for Doc to finish his story. Each did not want anyone else to hear the secrets that they shared.

"I suggested to the Claytons sending him off to a military boarding school after he tried to set fire to their bed one night after they went to sleep," Doc said. "Thank God they listened to me. Things just always seem to happen when he is around and it's never good. Nobody ever would actually see him do these things but we knew he did them. Diana would cry and beg me not to tell anyone. I last heard he was living in Las Vegas; don't know what he is doing but I'm sure he is up to no good! I reckon it's okay to share these things with ya'll 'cause it has been so long and all that is just water under the bridge... so to speak. Why do you ask, huh?"

Miss Mary punched Jazz so he wouldn't say anything. Jazz grunted. She did not want to alarm Doc about Mrs. Clayton.

"Well Doc, I was just wondering," Miss Mary said. "I knew that there was a story, but I didn't know exactly what it was."

With a deeply concerned look on his face, Doc inquired, "Are Charles and Diana okay? I always know that if something strange happens to those fine people I will seek the world over to find Johnny Clayton to bring some justice, huh?"

They stood in front of the elevators as Doc reached out with one of his elderly, shaking hands to push the down button.

Footsteps came decisively toward them.

"Mr. Barfield... I mean Dr. Barfield, now honestly. You doctor's make the worst patients. You have got to go back to your room," the head nurse demanded.

Miss Mary and Jazz stepped onto the elevator.

"Okay, I'm going to my room," Doc told the nurse. "Night folks," he said with a wave to friends. "Next time, we'll visit back home as long as we want to. Mary, call me and I can tell you more, huh?"

The elevator door closed as Jazz's bulging eyes of curiosity stared at Miss Mary. Her face indicated that she was in deep thought analyzing the situation.

CHAPTER TWENTY-SEVEN

EVEN THOUGH IT WAS another hot Saturday in
August with plenty for him to do, Jazz had a hard
time concentrating on his work. Mrs. Clayton was
on his mind.

Johnny was supposed to visit, but no one
had heard from nor seen him. Where was Mrs.
Clayton? What had Mr. Clayton done to his
Sweet Potato? All Jazz could do at this point was
trust The Greeter.

Miss Mary asked a few questions around
The Store, but this only made her out to be a nosy,
old woman. No one thought anything unusual
was going on — except Miss Mary and Jazz.

Everyone else thought Mr. and Mrs. Clayton
were aging. Old people often have personality
changes, so it was understandable when Mr.
Clayton talked a little short. As for Mrs. Clayton,
it was time for her to start staying at home.

Mr. Johnston was actually relieved she
stopped coming in The Store, because he was

concerned about her falling down and getting hurt. He had even told Miss Mary to mind her own business and remember her job was The Greeter.

Jazz overheard Mr. Johnston reprimanding Miss Mary concerning his feelings about Mrs. Clayton when he got to work. There was really nothing Jazz or Miss Mary could do but wait. He thought this was the longest week of his life because he truly did not know what was going on.

He was gathering up scattered carts from the parking lot when he spotted a car at the bank that looked like the Clayton's car. There were some carts that needed to be gathered at that end of the parking lot, so he ran over to that area.

Best he could tell, Mrs. Clayton was in the car! Just then, Mr. Clayton returned and got into his vehicle. As he pulled the car into the far end of the Wal-Mart parking lot, Jazz could see that it was indeed the Clayton's car.

Jazz thought he must have been in a hurry, because Mr. Clayton usually drove around until he found a parking space near the front door.

When Mr. Clayton got out of his car, he nearly ran to the front door of The Store. Jazz had never seen him move so fast. Mrs. Clayton sat motionless with her head hanging down while the car engine was running to keep the air condition on in the 102-degree weather.

Jazz yelled across the parking lot to Mrs. Clayton, but figured she couldn't hear him. He had a large number of carts he had gathered and needed to return to The Store. He would go speak to Mrs. Clayton, after he returned the carts.

He hoped she was taking a short nap and would be finished when he came back outside. Jazz felt it was a real shame she couldn't come into The Store she loved so dear.

"A day without Wal-Mart is like a day without sunshine," Sweet Potato had said many times. She always had a soft, sweet laugh, like a little child.

After he rapidly pushed the carts into The Store, Jazz overheard a conversation between the new Store photographer — who was originally from Madison, Georgia — and Miss Mary.

"Can you keep an eye on the photo studio for a minute? I have got to go to the bathroom," the photographer said. "I put up the sign that I will be back in 10 minutes but it shouldn't take me that long."

"Oh, yeah, by the way," the photographer said as she rushed off. "If somebody named Clayton comes in, his passport picture is ready. I know he is anxious to visit his relatives in Mexico City."

Jazz thoughts were discombobulated. Mexico City... Mexico City! The Claytons were from The Woods. They didn't know anything about Mexico City. Travel was never on their list of favorite activities — certainly not another country.

"Miss Mary! Miss Mary!" Jazz was out of

breath and almost in a panic to tell her that Mrs. Clayton was indeed still alive and out in the parking lot. Miss Mary just smiled and motioned at him to be silent as Sugar Pie entered The Store.

"Hello Charles," Miss Mary said as he passed.

There was no sign Mr. Clayton heard her. Jazz hoped Mr. Clayton had his mind on getting back to Mrs. Clayton.

Miss Mary moved closer to the entrance of The Store so she could see his reaction when he read the sign that the photographer would be back in 10 minutes. She could see the studio from her post. When Mr. Clayton approached the sign, he was noticeably angered by it and quickly turned and kept walking.

Jazz could wait no longer to tell The Greeter the good news. "Miss Mary, you are not going to believe this — Mrs. Clayton is alive! She is outside in the car. I know it must be at least 102 degrees out there, but Mr. Clayton was nice enough to roll up the windows and leave the air-conditioning on for her. I was planning on going back and speaking to her, want to come too?"

"Okay, Jazz, now I know this is hard to explain, but we have to act like nothing is going on. Trust me," Miss Mary said. "The Claytons are in serious trouble, but we must keep this between me and you. Understand?"

Jazz's young, innocent eyes believed her, but his heart felt finding Mrs. Clayton meant this was all over. How could The Claytons still be in trouble? Since when was Mr. Clayton in trouble?

"Go back out in the parking lot. Don't go over to the car, but just get close enough to check on Diana and then come back here as soon as possible. Be quick now," Miss Mary emphasized each word like it was an important step.

Jazz did not know what plan was already in motion, but he was glad to be a part of it.

He could see Mrs. Clayton was indeed in the car but she appeared to be slumped over as if she had fallen asleep, probably still taking a nap. She was old.

Jazz ran back in The Store. He almost stepped out in front of a car because he was so excited.

When he walked back in, Miss Mary was checking Mr. Clayton's bag. He looked anxious and ready to leave The Store.

"Have a good day! Oh Charles..." Miss Mary started. The man never turned or even acknowledged his name.

Miss Mary was busy doing her job. Jazz was in a tizzy.

"Miss Mary, what is going on?" The look on Jazz's face exposed his utter confusion.

"Don't worry Jazz. It will all work out," Miss Mary said. "I just hope we're not too late. Looks like it's time for my 15-minute break. I've been working long enough to get one. I'm going to make a phone call."

Jazz could hardly believe his ears. All this was going on and she decided now -- now of all times -- to go on a break. He took a deep breath and tried desperately to remind himself he trusted Miss Mary. He told himself she always did the right thing. He hoped, even prayed she was doing the right thing now.

CHAPTER TWENTY-EIGHT

MISS MARY'S BREAK seemed to last forever. The Claytons drove off shortly after her break started. Jazz was so anxious to find out what was going on, he brought in carts one at a time. He truly hoped Mr. Johnston did not see him doing this. Finally, Miss Mary returned, as if nothing was going on.

"Jazz, I want you to stay out in the parking lot until you see Mr. Clayton drive up. Come back in and let me know," she instructed. "Don't run. I don't want him to notice anything different."

Jazz shook his head in agreement, but with disbelief.

"Miss Mary, Mr. Clayton just left The Store," Jazz told her. "Why would he come back?"

"He's coming back. You'll see. I've just got a feeling," Miss Mary said with conviction.

Jazz smiled and walked away. Miss Mary had feelings, powerful feelings indeed. He knew better than to say anything about her feelings.

Jazz continued about his normal business in the parking lot. He gathered long rows of carts, which he pushed with all of his might back into The Store. This method kept him outside longer, but he was quickly running out of carts.

It had been 30 minutes since he talked with Miss Mary. He collected another long line of carts. Just as he was about to push the carts across the street, out of nowhere someone jumped right in his face and shoved him on the shoulder.

"Hey Jazz," Josh began yelling. "Is it true what Rose Wilder's daughter, Heather, is saying about you? I want to know if it is."

Heather usually did not have much to say, but had been known from time to time to tell a tall tale for attention.

Suddenly, the Clayton vehicle careened into the parking lot and halted in a space close to The Store. This time he was alone. Jazz spotted the car and tried to get the carts at least across the street. He was desperately trying to get to Miss Mary to warn her.

"Well? Cat got ya tongue? Is it true?" The bully would not let up on Jazz. Josh pushed his shoulder with one hand again.

"Look Josh," Jazz sternly said. "We're not children anymore, so you can get out of my face. I have a job to do right now. Something you would not know anything about."

Joshua was so shocked he pulled his head

back and did a mocking face. Jazz literally ran as fast as he could to get the carts to the short door. He wasn't able to get the carts inside, but by some miracle he was able to get to Miss Mary before Mr. Clayton entered The Store. Jazz began to motion to her.

As soon as Miss Mary saw Jazz, she pulled out her cell phone and hit one number.

"Go, go, it's safe," Miss Mary said into the phone. "Tell them to go now!"

Jazz wondered who she was talking to.

Mr. Johnston turned the corner just in time to see her talking on her cell phone — a big no-no at work.

"Mary, you know..." Mr. Johnston began.

Mr. Clayton entered The Store. Jazz's head was spinning as he tried to watch all the action.

"Not now, Mr. Johnston. We can discuss this later, but trust me this is not the right time," Miss Mary interrupted.

Mr. Johnston appeared to be slightly annoyed by her and asked Miss Mary to step inside The Store. She followed to get a better view of Mr. Clayton. Although this appeared to be a friendly conversation, Miss Mary wasn't listening and kept looking around Mr. Johnston at the registers. She knew Mr. Clayton had returned to buy a specific item.

Miss Mary suddenly spotted him. Sugar Pie made a small purchase at register Number 1, the express lane. Then, Miss Mary and Mr. Clayton began walking toward the photography studio.

Jazz was in close pursuit.

"Come back here this instance, I'm not finished with you! Why are you leaving your post? Have you forgotten you are The Greeter? Jazz, son, I have warned you for the last time," Mr. Johnston's voice seemed to draw a crowd but his words faded into the distance as Miss Mary approached the photo counter.

"Sheriff Rowe! Arrest this man," Miss Mary said while pointing at Mr. Clayton. Sheriff Rowe came from the back of the photo studio area. The crowd seemed to become quite large.

"Mary, you have gone too far this time. I am going to have to ask you to turn in your vest immediately! This is absurd! This time you have gone way too far," Mr. Johnston said extremely loud.

Miss Mary stood up taller and prouder as she confidently straightened her clothes, including her blue vest.

"This is not Charles Clayton," Miss Mary announced as she boldly reached over and jerked off the wig that had been strategically glued to his head.

The trapped man yelped. He looked around quickly for an exit, but he was cornered in the studio like a wild mountain lion. There was no escape.

Miss Mary began to explain his diabolical plot, "This is Johnny Clayton — adopted son of

Mr. and Mrs. Clayton. He was adopted by them when his parents were killed in a car accident. Or was it an accident, Johnny? Diana Clayton is Johnny's aunt. His mother and Diana were sisters.

"The Claytons lovingly took him in as the son they never had, but it was never enough for Johnny. Bad things always seemed to happen whenever Johnny was around. So his adopted parents decided early to send him to a military boarding school."

Someone yelled out from the crowd, "But Mary, how did you figure out that this is Johnny?"

"Well, being The Greeter, people share a lot of information with me. Some folks think I'm nosy, but I'm a great listener. The Claytons had been telling me Johnny was coming to visit then, they stopped talking about him at the same time Diana quit coming into The Store she loves so much.

"Ever since we opened those doors The Claytons have come in every afternoon about the same time, until recently. Then, Charles' personality started getting abrupt. I wasn't sure of what to think at first.

"I thought since both Charles and Diana were diabetic this might have something to do with it, because they would only get a week's worth of medication at a time. They both came in every Tuesday for a refill. They haven't been coming in and getting their medicine for several weeks.

"I also found out Johnny lived in Las

Vegas and I figured out he got into some trouble with some illegal betting. He ran up a hefty bill, too. Didn't you Johnny?"

Johnny stood with his head hanging in shame.

"You can't change the spots on a leopard," Miss Mary continued. "Being in such desperate financial disaster, he decided to visit his aunt and uncle. This is why he couldn't give a specific date for his arrival to them. He wanted them to know he was coming but he didn't want them to know when! Didn't want anyone to follow him or trace his calls. Diana told me he was calling them collect on payphones.

"Johnny knew they have a sizable amount of money because he is listed as their sole benefactor. They had told me everything was going to their only son when they died. I am the executrix for their wills. Only Johnny couldn't wait. He needed the money and a passport as well to leave the country before the people he owed the money to found him.

"Here's the best part — Johnny is well known in Las Vegas. Charles and Diana did not know what he did but they knew that he was in the entertainment business. He is an impersonator — a very good impersonator!"

Miss Vera from the bakery had pushed her way up to the front of the crowd. "Go on Mary, but how did you know he is an impersonator?"

"Good question, Vera," Miss Mary agreed.

"I'm getting there. You see people might not think much of us Door Greeters, but Sam Walton had a great concept when he invented our jobs. We form relationships with our customers like family. Why even little children think of us like a grandmother."

Conner and Matilda inched their way through the crowd to give MeMe a much needed hug as she continued her story. Then, they returned to their mother.

"Johnny stayed home with Diana," Miss Mary explained. "He would send Charles into The Store to gather up certain items neither Charles nor Diana would need or even want. Then, I began to notice Charles was not always Charles. As part of my job, I have to look into the bags to check the purchases against the sales receipt, for instance, toothpaste, toothbrush and dental floss. I thought this was odd because both the Claytons have dentures and buy a tablet cleanser for false teeth."

Miss Mary took a big, deep breath.

"Johnny always put the receipt in his wallet," she said. "So when he would exit The Store and I would ask to see his receipt, he would open his wallet. I noticed a large amount of lottery tickets as well as several Las Vegas dancers' pictures.

This is when I realized it was not Charles, and Johnny is here trying to escape a gambling debt. Also, Charles and Diana told me numerous times over the years they never gambled and hated traveling so I knew they certainly had not been to Las Vegas.

"One day in his wallet, I saw a professional picture of someone dressed up in a beautiful sequined evening gown looking like Elizabeth Taylor. The name Jo-Jo Cannon was printed on it. I had heard entertainers sometimes choose their show name based on their favorite pet's name and their mother's maiden name.

"I remembered the Claytons had a poodle named Jo-Jo when Johnny was little and his mother's maiden name was Cannon. Also, these were not items that you would see in Charles' wallet. I know because he too would often place his receipt there so I would see what he carried in his billfold. Charles had his driver's license and a laminated card with The Lord's Prayer on one side and The Prayer of Jabez on the other.

"So like putting pieces of a puzzle together I soon deducted that Jo-Jo is Johnny Clayton, a professional impersonator. Although this impersonation didn't take much work because he already looks like a younger version of his Uncle Charles," Miss Mary finished.

Miss Vera wanted more details. "Okay, but how did you know Charles was Johnny today and that he was going to be in The Store at this time for you to call Sheriff Rowe over here and that he would go to the photography studio?"

"Well, those are great questions. Earlier, Jazz noticed The Claytons left the bank and

Charles drove over here. Johnny hasn't been allowing The Clayton's to take their medication for their diabetes on a regular basis, so they're like zombies. Both of them told me on several occasions that if they did not take their medication and eat on time they felt like they were in a fog — tired and sleepy.

"Mr. Clayton stayed home today, while Johnny went to the bank and signed his name. He kept her in the car and told the bank teller she was not feeling well. He then took out the appropriate paper work and scribbled Mrs. Clayton's signature onto the bank card. Johnny needed both signatures. The signature at that point was not that important, because everyone at the bank could see Mrs. Clayton sitting out in the car. The money had been delivered at the bank, because I noticed the Wells Fargo truck up from Augusta was over there when I was coming into work today. Last, I found out he was planning on leaving for Mexico City, because he had his passport pictures taken here and was coming to pick them up.

"So, Johnny conveniently took Diana home and returned. I knew he would be coming back to The Store as soon as possible for two reasons — Johnny needed to pick up his passport pictures dressed like Charles Clayton. The authorities would not be looking for Charles Clayton. They would be looking for Johnny Clayton, the Las Vegas entertainer and impersonator, also known as Jo-Jo Cannon!

"He was planning on traveling as Charles Clayton. Also, he needed a lock for his briefcase with all of the money. Johnnie purchased a briefcase last week and a lock earlier today, but as he was leaving and I checked his bags, the key fell off of the lock and onto my left shoe. I called his name to give it to him but he never did turn around.

"That was when I knew for sure he was not used to being called Charles. One thing about the real Charles Clayton, he had no problem hearing. Diana told me before she often wished he did though."

The crowd laughed slightly.

"When he discovered that his lock had no key, instead of coming back and asking if I found the lock or going to customer service he decided it would be better and faster to buy another lock and key," Miss Mary explained.

"How're the Claytons doing? Where are they?" Mr. Roberto yelled, interrupting Miss Mary as Sheriff Rowe placed the handcuffs on the accused wrists. Johnny was looking very disgusted at this time.

"More good questions," Miss Mary said. "I'm getting there. Johnny wasn't actually going to kill The Claytons. After all, they are the only real parents he has. Right, Johnny? He was just going to leave them in their house until someone either missed them or found them, dead or alive.

"Either way he would be gone with the

money and in another country. Still no one would be looking for him, because no one knew that Johnny was here in The Woods.

"I knew they were at their home being held hostage, because no one was being allowed into the Clayton home. I know, I tried to visit them several times and so did the Sheriff. When I realized Johnny was going to return to The Store today, I told Jazz to let me know as soon as he saw him -- I mean Johnny dressed as Charles -- get out of his car.

"I had called Christy Rowe the dispatch operator for our local emergency number, 911 and told her the situation. Her husband Sheriff Rowe was dispatched to come over to wait in the photography studio for Johnny. As soon as Jazz told me Johnny was back here in The Store's parking lot, I called Christy and told her it would be safe for the EMTs to go into The Clayton home to check on them.

"Since they have diabetes, this constitutes a medical emergency. The EMTs had been waiting down the street for my call, which I did right before telling Sheriff Rowe who to arrest."

"How did you suspect it was Johnny?" Miss Vera asked the question on everybody's mind.

"Well… Jazz and I went to visit Doc in the hospital. Doc told us that Johnny was nothing but bad news. The Claytons have been telling me for months that Johnny was coming to visit and then nothing! They suddenly stopped mentioning him at the same time Mrs. Clayton stopped coming in The Store. Diana did not want anyone to know the trouble Johnny was years ago. I didn't know until I visited Doc in the hospital," Miss Mary said.

"So Jazz was in on this? He helped solve this Woods' mystery and save The Claytons' lives as well as all of their money?" Miss Vera blurted out with great surprise on her face.

"He most certainly did," Miss Mary said with pride. "Jazz is very smart. When he came running in today to tell me Diana was out in the parking lot but all the windows were rolled up and the air-conditioning was on, I knew she was just barely alive and that Charles must have been at home today either tied up, sick or both. She likes her window rolled down no matter what the weather is. Let's all give Jazz a round of applause."

Jazz was shocked at Miss Mary's story. He could see how she put all of the little pieces of the puzzle together. Once again, he thought she was brilliant and had a way of making him feel like the greatest person in the world. His face turned red as he put his head down.

It seemed like the whole town was in Wal-Mart praising Jazz.

"Let's give The Greeter a great, big round of applause, too," Andy chimed in. "She some-how always seems to save the day!"

"Okay! Everyone disperse here. The show's

over. Everyone back to work. Break it up. We have a great sale going on today in electronics. Check the falling prices in baby supplies too. Mary, back to the door. Everyone continue shopping. Glad you are here," Mr. Johnston said, not pleased at the ruckus created by this unbelievable story.

"Not until we get a picture of Miss Mary, Jazz and Mr. Clayton... I mean Johnny," said The Store photographer — also a reporter for the Evanston Times.

"By the way, Mr. Johnston was in on this as well. That's why he brought me into The Store when Johnny returned so he must be in the picture, too," Miss Mary said.

Mr. Johnston acknowledged by nodding his head. He was speechless, but appreciated the fact Miss Mary had made him look great in front of the customers as well as the other employees.

After the pictures were quickly taken, Mr. Johnston started to walk off.

"Mr. Johnston? Mr. Johnston?" Miss Mary tried to get his attention. "Do you want my vest now or later?"

"Go back to work!" he stated rather abruptly as he was walking away.

Miss Mary got the last laugh, at least this time.

The crowd was still hanging around to see what other exciting announcements Miss Mary might have. Two other officers appeared pushing through the crowd to help take Johnny into custody.

At that moment, Miss Mary's cell phone rang and she answered it.

"Hello? Yes… Yes… Yes… Oh thank God," Miss Mary said. "By the way, can you tell the EMTs to check the Claytons' wrists? Johnny had to tie their arms together with ropes to keep them at the house when he first started leaving both of them alone together. Thanks again and thanks for trusting me. See you later. You and the sheriff are the best!"

Everyone waited without a word; they wanted to know who was calling.

"That was the dispatch operator, Christy, calling to let us all know the Claytons are going to be okay," Miss Mary reported. "The Emergency Medical Team is going to be taking them over to MCG hospital in Augusta — at least for an overnight stay — to make sure they get their medication started back on a good schedule. I guess they can visit Doc while they're over there.

"A while back, Diana said she would only let Doc look at her medical condition, so this way she will get her wish."

Everyone laughed then they began remembering why they came to The Store in the first place.

Suddenly, Miss Vera yelled out one last question, "Okay, how did you know about the Claytons' wrists?"

"Well, the first time I knew for sure Johnny came in The Store, he bought some rope. When I checked his bag that day he was very anxious," Miss Mary explained. "He hurried out without even talking to me. The Claytons are so nice, they always stopped and talked whenever they were in The Store. Both of them explained why they made each purchase.

"The next time I saw the real Mr. Clayton in The Store, he was nervously asking the pharmacist what he could put on abrasive skin. After Diana started falling down, she was not scraping her skin, but bruises would appear. She showed them to me several times. So I knew that the rope was being used to tie them up and Charles was concerned about his wife."

The officers were starting to take Johnny out of the building, but not until Miss Mary gave him a piece of her mind.

"As for you young man," she started. "What you did is terribly wrong. I guess the moral of this story is one that they did not teach you in impersonator school, which is 'Don't ever impersonate someone with false teeth when you have real teeth!'"

The crowd that had been walking away returned, but only to shake their heads in agreement and give a short laugh or smirk.

As Johnny was leaving, he looked like he had gathered his second wind. "Old woman, this isn't over," he said with a grimace. "My plan was brilliant but you had to come along with your nosy old self and mess up everything. You'll see. I will return to see you again... when you least expect it. You better be looking over your shoulder you old bat because you won't even know what I will look like when I do!"

CHAPTER TWENTY-NINE

THE WOODS SAW another Labor Day coming up. The children had returned to school. Bob, the Builder, a children's character, was in The Store's parking lot building a dog house.

Conner, Mathilda and Harry Stillwell, IV were there to help their favorite character. The theme song was playing and all the children were singing. Conner sang the loudest.

Harry's eye had cleared up, just like Doc said it would, and now Harry was dealing with a broken arm Doc had set for him. Harry's grandmother, Mrs. Stillwell, told The Greeter she was so thankful for Doc and his common sense approach to medicine.

Doc had given Mrs. Stillwell a plastic bread bag to wrap around the cast when the boy bathed at night so as not to get the cast wet.

The end of summer had come to The Woods, but discontent was in the air on that September day. Jazz hoped that a little cool weather was on the way.

The Greeter was at work doing a super job as usual. Since last month, Miss Mary and Jazz, along with Mr. Johnston in the background, were on the front page of the Evanston Times. There was talk some reporter from The Augusta Chronicle was also coming to do a story on them. Everybody for miles around came into The Store just to talk with Miss Mary and to have their picture taken with the mystery solver.

Jazz was pushing carts when Marsha Jean seemed to fly out of nowhere and ran into him. She almost knocked him down.

"Good Morning, Marsha Jean," Jazz said. "How are you doing?" He quickly decided to maintain a nice, pleasant tone even though he almost landed on his face. He was also proud of himself for being able to talk.

"Sorry about that. Don't have time to talk Jes-abe. I have to go home," Marsha Jean blurted out as she kept running to her car.

Everyone could hear her emergency alarm go off on her car as she hit the wrong button on her key ring. Jazz ran to her side as she desperately tried to get the alarm to stop. He wanted to help her in any way he could. He had to talk rather loudly to be heard over the car alarm. "Marsha Jean, what's wrong? Can I..."

Marsha Jean repeated herself, but with more intensity in her voice, "Don't have time to talk Jes-abe. I have to go home. Something terrible has happened."

As she finally got the alarm to cease, she unlocked the doors, got in her car and sped off. Jazz hoped everything was okay with the Hollingsworth family, but from Marsha Jean's reaction he feared the worse.

Since it was Saturday — the busiest day of the week at The Store — he turned his mind back to his own work. There were plenty of carts to be returned inside for the shoppers.

He also needed to repair two of the cart corrals. The carts were often shoved into the corrals so hard that screws needed tightening up on occasion. He decided to think about Marsha Jean later. It wasn't long before Jazz had his own set of problems to be concerned about though.

"You-hoo...Yeah, I's talking to you. Mr. Jazzy, Jazz... Mr. J... You think that you're the town ce-le-bri-ty since you had ya picture on the front page of the paper," Joshua mocked. "Well, I got a news flash for you, ya best be leaving my girlfriend alone. Heather Wilder belongs to me. Gotta tattoo on my arm that says so."

Joshua T. Taylor was back. He rolled up his old faded out black Ozzie Osborne t-shirt sleeve to show what looked like an ink pen had scratched something into his arm — Hether.

Jazz thought of him like bad breath — no matter what you do, halitosis comes back, just like Joshua.

The bully swaggered up to Jazz and continued to yell, "She says that you are the daddy to her baby," Joshua yelled. "They say that with a blood sample you can do something called D-N-A testing to find out whose baby it is. Well, I am here to get that blood sample!"

Josh began to do a little shuffle type of a dance around Jazz. This reminded Jazz of an old crusty character named Ernest T. Bass from The Andy Griffith Show. He had seen the re-runs on television at Miss Mary's house.

While thinking about the similarities and the tattoo, a smirk crept across his face, but suddenly dissipated. Joshua was big, weighing around 240 pounds, and mean. He did not mind picking a fight and scraping with anybody at anytime.

"Well, is it your baby?"

Jazz had no idea what Josh was talking about. Knowing the bully the way Jazz did, he probably had gotten this story all confused with some other gossip.

"No, not my baby Josh. I ain't ever been with Heather. She's a nice girl, but…"

Jazz knew he had just said too much -- way too much. He knew Heather's mother, Rose, had a bad reputation, but Heather was a good girl. Joshua could only dream about Heather as a girlfriend.

"I guess she's been real nice to ya, yeah? Is that whatcha saying? She certainly ain't done nothing with me," Josh said as he continued his

Ernest T. Bass shuffle. Jazz felt like there was no way out of this free-for-all.

Then, suddenly a miracle happened; Sheriff Rowe came driving up in one of the two county patrol cars.

"What seems to be going on here?" Sheriff Rowe said. "Jazz, are you all right?"

He nodded. He was really glad to see the sheriff.

Over the dispatch, the calm voice of his wife, Christy, could be heard.

"We have found signs of buried bones out back of the Hollingsworth residence, near the stable, possible homicide. I need to send both patrol cars out to the premises to start the investigation. The crime lab in Atlanta has been notified at this time. We are to make sure that the site is secured."

Sheriff Rowe acknowledged the message.

Jazz was in shock! He could not believe what he just heard — a dead body at Marsha Jean's house? How could this be?

"Sheriff Rowe, remember we had a 911 call a little while ago to Route 4 off of Cumberland Woods Drive," the dispatcher said. "An ambulance was requested. Can you do a back-up on that call before going out to the Hollingsworth place?"

Again, Sheriff Rowe signaled that he had heard the dispatcher.

Jazz was frozen. He truly could not believe

his ears.

"Gentlemen, I suggest you discuss your differences like men. I have to go on another call now. Joshua, you still have some explaining to do about the money that was missing from the coach's desk. The next time…"

"Sheriff," Jazz's voice was shaking, he was almost in tears. "I live at Route 4 off of Cumberland Woods Drive."

He wished with all of his heart he didn't live there, but he did.

"Get in son. I'll give you a ride over there." Jazz did as he was told, not thinking of the consequences of leaving The Store at the time.

During the ride, Sheriff dispatched Christy and requested she call Miss Mary to let Mr. Johnston know there was an emergency with a request for an ambulance at Jazz's house. All the way home, Jazz just knew his father was dead.

He did not know what a heart attack felt like but he thought he was experiencing one now. The drive to his house was only a few minutes from The Store, but it felt like it took a long time.

When the sheriff pulled into the driveway, Jazz did not wait for the car to fully stop. He jumped out and immediately leapt up on the front porch of the place he called home.

He imagined sitting with his father on those steps learning how to bait a fishing pole when he was barely four and five years old.

There was the front porch swing where his

daddy would often take him to have a little talk about different things when mother did not need to be involved. He remembered the day Mrs. Turnbow brought Wal-do home and Jazz was pleasantly surprised that afternoon to see the four-legged family member waiting on him.

Wal-do was no where to be seen. Something was terribly wrong for the dog not to greet Jazz. He flung the squeaky screen door open; it was barely hanging on its hinges.

The door had been like this ever since daddy had gotten sick and was too ill to fix it. Jazz remembered his dad saying time and time again: "I'll work on that door tomorrow when I feel better, son. Gimme something to look forward to, so don't be doing my job."

The front wooden door was wide open. His folks would never leave the door like that unless they had to leave in an emergency. He ran straight through the house directly to Robert's room, only to find that no one was there. Their favorite Bluegrass song was blaring loudly, the one that he and Robert loved to hear so much - "I am a Man of Constant Sorrow."

With lightening motion, Jazz turned off the radio. Then, all he could hear was the blur-blur sound of the two floor fans in the house.

"Dad? Sam?" His desperate cries were only heard by the echo of his own voice on the freshly polished wooden floors.

Miss Mary had realized the house needed

a woman's touch and was now devoting a day a week to clean, cook and visit with Robert. That was all over now.

Jazz ran back through the sitting area as he heard the phone ringing in the kitchen. He thought it must be his dad or Sam to let him know what was going on and that everything was going to be all right. He apprehensively picked up the phone, "He... hello?"

He could hear sobbing at the other end of the line. It was a female. His heart sank; he just knew that it was Sam calling with terrible news. "Sam? What is…"

"This is not Sam," a woman said as the crying continued. Jazz did not know what to think or say. He remained quiet, as he heard screaming in the background.

"This is Aunt Inez, please let me talk to my brother. Is Bubba there? Is Bubba there? Oh God… this must be a nightmare that I am in! Please dear God someone help me!"

Jazz did not recognize the voice, but the person identified herself as his aunt. The three month old baby was screaming in the background along with everyone else at Aunt Inez's house.

"Jazz, please… Oh, Lord… someone help me," continued his Aunt Inez's cries.

"Robert isn't here right now. I've got to go! Please call back later," Jazz said as he fought back his own tears. His Aunt Inez always seemed to call for no reason and could truly make a mountain out of a mole hill.

"Carl has been killed! I got to talk to Bubba! Please! Dear God, Jazz, put him on the phone, now!"

Jazz did not know what to say. Uncle Carl was dead, murdered? Had the whole world gone crazy at once? He gently let the receiver go; it swung up against the kitchen wall.

Jazz could not talk and even if he could what would he have said. He did not have the words to tell Aunt Inez her brother was dead.

The cart pusher did not know what to do. He wished for it all to go away, he wanted to escape from all of his problems just as he turned away from the dangling phone line. He looked out the kitchen window into the back yard and saw the sun fading as he felt like his spirit was too.

"Jazz... God! Please someone help me! Robert, are you there? Carl is dead!"

CHAPTER THIRTY

IT WAS ON A SATURDAY morning in October when Jazz finally heard some good news.

He stepped through the grand entrance of The Store where Miss Mary hugged him, and announced, "Jazz, Jazz… Oh happy day! They found a heart for Matthew! Angel Flight is on its way to transport him." She was bursting with jubilation.

Now, Jazz's mind raced with all sorts of thoughts. He thought about the memorial service and Marsha Jean. His mind was a little foggy today, more than usual — he had been up late most of the night before with the baby.

Aunt Inez and her five children moved in with them after Uncle Carl died, disappeared or went missing — no one knew for sure.

She was a good mother, but when it came to sleeping, a tornado could not wake her up. Therefore, Jazz and Sam took turns listening out for the children, as well as for their Robert.

The baby, Carly, had taken a shine to Jazz, and the feeling was mutual. He didn't mind rocking her until the sun came up.

Most folks, like Jazz and Sam, silently believed Aunt Inez and her children were much better off without a drinking man with a mean streak.

The life insurance had not paid out because Carl's body hadn't been found, at least not yet. Mr. Clayton told them to not worry — it would all work out so the benefits of the policy would be paid out. The waiting period for a missing person to be declared dead was usually a year.

Aunt Inez had searched desperately for Uncle Carl. Everyone knew he had always been a drinker. His guzzling buddies hung out with him for a couple of days here or there, but never this long. He had been gone for two weeks.

When his family had not seen hide nor hair of him in three weeks, Aunt Inez and the children searched everywhere she thought Uncle Carl might have gone.

After combing Jacksonville and the surrounding areas, she put her family in the car around midnight on a Friday. Aunt Inez drove all night long. When the children woke up the next morning, they searched Harlem, Georgia — because Uncle Carl claimed he was related to

Hardy of the famous Laurel and Hardy comedy duo. He wasn't there.

Next, she hit U.S. Interstate 20 and cruised west up to Social Circle, Georgia, but didn't find him. However, the family ate a great lunch at The Blue Willow Inn before driving to Lincolnton, Georgia, where she thought some of his old football buddies might know his whereabouts.

She swung through Augusta to talk to some of the folks in the art community because Uncle Carl lived there briefly when he was a medical illustrator.

While in Augusta, Aunt Inez called a dear old friend and professor who taught at Augusta State University. They met downtown at Mally's Bagels and Grits.

The children loved the raisin bagels with cinnamon and walnut cream cheese spread and were wrestling over the four bags of bagel chips before they even left the parking lot. Aunt Inez couldn't resist a quick trip through the Morris Museum, too, since she was so close. Though her husband was missing, she still wanted her children to enjoy their trip. The museum always portrayed the finest southern art and culture.

On their way up Broad Street, Aunt Inez made a stop at Hot Foods by Calvin. No self-respecting southerner could pass through Augusta without eating at Calvin's.

The family wound up in Statesboro, Georgia, thinking Uncle Carl might visit some relatives. Two of his cousins taught at Georgia Southern University. One of them offered Aunt Inez and her children a safe haven for the night. In the morning, they still hadn't found Uncle Carl.

About two o'clock that Sunday morning, one of her neighbors in Jacksonville — Mrs. MacIntyre — called Aunt Inez's cell phone. The friend always watched the house when they went out of town.

The dogs had their own door, so they could go in and out as they wanted to. However, Mrs. MacIntyre said the dogs were barking real loud — she thought they had trapped a fox or something.

About an hour later, Aunt Inez called Mrs. MacIntyre back to make sure everything was all right — hoping that Uncle Carl had come home.

As soon as Mrs. MacIntyre said hello, Aunt Inez could hear voices in the background and knew that something was wrong. A police officer got on the phone and told her to return home as soon as possible. She was so excited — she just knew Uncle Carl had been found.

An exhausted Aunt Inez, along with her five children, arrived home around 10 a.m. to discover police cars parked in the driveway and officers running around the house and yard.

Yellow plastic "Do not cross" streamers were wrapped all the way around Aunt Inez's house. The police believed foul play had occurred. As soon as she parked the car, she searched for Uncle Carl. He wasn't at home.

Forensic investigators had already arrived to examine droplets of blood found on the sidewalk, up the back porch steps and throughout the kitchen. The crimson spots led back out through the garage.

Before anyone could talk to the family, Aunt Inez saw blood droplets and screamed. "What have ya'll done to my husband?"

Not too long after this horrific moment, Aunt Inez called her Bubba.

Mrs. MacIntyre told Inez and the police she heard a ruckus in the neighbor's back yard. At first she thought it was a wild animal exciting the dogs. Once she got her eyes focused, she could see Carl being forcefully carried into the house by two men.

The chief investigator told her they needed something for DNA testing so they could be sure it was Uncle Carl's blood — such as hair from a comb.

Nothing was missing from the house, except the green 1997 Bonneville. All of the jewelry and other valuables were still there, yet the house was a mess. Clothes were thrown everywhere as if someone looked for something specific.

Aunt Inez knew something had gone awry, but didn't know why. She was scared, not only for her life, but also for her children.

Police ruled out Aunt Inez as a suspect early in this case, since she was out of town during the incident. She told detectives her plan, got in the van and drove to Evanston. Aunt Inez called her brother from a payphone, and then drove as fast as she safely could with the children and the dogs.

Aunt Inez had picked up many stray animals throughout the years and found them great homes. However, two dogs stayed with her. One, a basset hound named Huckleberry, barked all night if he was left outside. The other dog, a golden retriever mix, only had one ear and answered to Van Gogh.

Once the family came to Evanston, Wal-do loved the company of the other dogs and relished attention from the children. Jazz and Sam were excited about these house guests because their dad was so exuberant.

After last month's scare that put Robert in the hospital for four days, he seemed to be feeling better when he returned home. Having his sister's family in the house sure did put a smile on his face.

Jazz was home the day Aunt Inez received the call that the DNA report returned with a 95 percent assurance the blood and the hair sample matched. The investigator told her that in similar cases the missing person usually was not found alive. Aunt Inez thought she was going to die when she heard this, but she had to be strong for the children.

With her worst nightmare all but confirmed,

she felt it was time for her and the children to move on with a life that would not include Carl. He had vanished six weeks earlier. She decided to have a memorial service, a ceremony to honor her husband and give the family closure.

Uncle Carl's memorial service was beautiful as far as services go, Jazz thought. Aunt Inez invited a few friends and ran an obituary announcement back in The Jacksonville Chronicle, as well as one in The Evanston Times.

The Reverend Bentley gave a miraculous talk on while we do not always understand the reason — we must accept there was one.

Since Uncle Carl did not go to church much, but he loved the outdoors, Jazz suggested having the service at the bird sanctuary. Aunt Inez went to The Store and bought a beautiful picture frame to hold the most recent picture she had of Uncle Carl. The children were dressed very well for the ceremony.

Everyone stood for the 15-minute requiem. Miss Vera recited an elegy she wrote for the sad occasion. Miss Mary crooned an a capella version of "Amazing Grace." Aunt Inez was supposed to say a few words, but she got all choked up, then buried her face in her right hand while she held baby Carly on her left hip.

Each of the children said something, except Carly. "He was our daddy and we loved him," was the gist of their comments. All of them had drawn a picture and colored it just for their dad.

As soon as the family ended their eulogies, the Reverend Bentley spoke.

"Yes, indeed my friends, Carl was loved by his family, friends and his Lord. Let's bow our heads in prayer to a most merciful God," the preacher said. After his prayer, the reverend read a few scriptures and gave a short uplifting message. It was appropriate, under the circumstances. This was followed by Mama Sugar singing a moving rendition of "Soon and Very Soon" by Andrea Crouch. Everyone was emotionally touched by the time she concluded.

The preacher closed with a brief, yet very effective prayer. Afterwards, he went over to the family and offered his continuous prayers and support. He wanted to know if the family needed anything.

Following the humble service, they all returned to Robert's home. It was filled with a great deal of food that would not take away the pain of a family without a husband and a father.

Jazz's other thoughts were about Marsha Jean. She had postponed going off to school because of the situation where the bones and remains had been discovered out at her family's plantation.

Dr. Cummings had encouraged her and Jazz to take some online college courses. The credits would be transferable, so if anyone wanted to go to another school they could.

Marsha Jean was enrolled in three classes

and enjoyed learning through Baker Online College. Next term, she planned to take Psychology 101 with Dr. Cummings as the instructor. Both Dr. Cummings and Marsha Jean had been encouraging Jazz to also take the psychology class.

"Jazz, take just one class and see if you like it. You are smart," Dr. Cummings said. "Marsha Jean is going to be in that class as well. You could be buddies. You can do your online work over at the Main Street library together. I'm pretty sure I can help you find some financial aid. I know Wal-Mart provides scholarships."

Jazz felt like somebody. He was seriously considering it. The cart pusher was now back out in the parking lot looking up at the mid-morning September sky and it appeared that rain was on the way, possibly a thunderstorm.

His thoughts were interrupted by the roar of a car engine passing by.

"Hey Jazz," yelled Marsha Jean in her brand new, gold Lexus. Her Beetle had been stolen and wrecked at the end of last month. She told Jazz and Miss Mary the whole terrible story.

Sheriff Rowe had found none other than Joshua, the bully himself, in her car early one Sunday morning. Joshua was all right but he had run off the side of the road into a tree.

Before he could get himself together, the sheriff just happened to be doing his rounds in that area. He stopped the patrol car, walked over and tapped on the driver's window.

Joshua tried to say Marsha Jean had let him borrow the car, but the sheriff was able to clear up the whole matter with a phone call to the Hollingsworth house. Marsha Jean was asleep. Mr. Hollingsworth looked and could not find the car in any of the garages.

Sheriff Rowe apologized for calling so early and went out to the mansion the next day to file the necessary report.

Fortunately, her dad had just ordered a brand, new gold, metallic four-door Lexus as a spare car, it arrived two days before this joyride. He just handed her the keys because he did not think that he would be driving it. She was grateful, but she really wanted her old Beetle back.

As Marsha Jean got out of her shiny, new car, she briskly walked toward The Store. Jazz just happened to be pushing the carts back in the short door and was able to catch up with her. The FBI report was supposed to be back so he thought she would know by now whose bones were buried out at her family's place.

Jazz had entertained the thought it would be bizarre if they were somehow Uncle Carl's remains, but he quickly dismissed this ridiculous idea.

"Stop by my department today when you go on break. There's something real important I want to talk to you about, okay?" Marsha Jean hurriedly said. She acted like she was running late to clock in.

The sun was shining in his face. Jazz could no longer see her. He could not answer her, so he waved and shook his head yes. His beautiful, brownish blonde hair was hanging in his eyes so he reached up with his right hand to sweep it to one side.

Jazz thought to himself: "Oh, no! Here we go again." His thoughts were intermingled with so many issues. He decided to think about Marsha Jean later, although he would indeed attempt to talk to her during his break.

For now Jazz was thinking his life ahead was filled with uncertainty, but he took comfort in knowing that he was safe and at his favorite place, his refuge — The Store.

In his mind, he heard Genesis singing "How Could I Ask for More?" His world was gently engulfed by all of his favorite people and surroundings as well as the most familiar sound of all.

The clanging of the shopping carts hitting together in the cart corral could be heard at least a half a mile away. As it had done all over the country, The Store breathed new life and hope into the town.

Wal-Mart was the life's blood of the community.

AUTHOR'S NOTES

Dear Reader:

I'm glad you are here! I wanted to share a few thoughts with you.

Have you ever been treated unfairly? At some point or another I think we all have -- whether through family life, a boss, an institution or problems we may have unknowingly caused for ourselves.

The characters as well as the plot in *The Greeter* show various examples of injustice. Jazz shows us that life doesn't always deal us a winning hand. Life is uncertain. Yet, we can overcome insurmountable odds with hope.

This is no more evident than through Jazz. Jazz is all of us. He represents the pride we take in our first job. Most of us can relate to his repetitive job. We often do the same things over and over again.

Sometimes, we lose sight of our job's meaning. Jazz finds meaning for his and understands how it fits into the big picture of The Store.

Do you ever feel like you're outside looking in on the party? This is illustrated through Jazz working mainly in the parking lot, but he is allowed, so to speak, to visit the party from time to time by going inside The Store.

Jazz has problems that seem to come at him from all angles, like Job in the Bible. We all need hope -- for Jazz it's found through the guidance and encouragement of Miss Mary.

Her job is not just a job, she offers each person who enters the grand entrance a human factor, a spiritual connection to your shopping experience. She is the heroine of the story.

I hope you enjoyed *The Greeter*. It's about you -- it's about people. It's a book from the little person's perspective.

I'd love to hear from you! Visit my Web site at www.thegreeterbook.com and send me e-mail at drmecooper@drmecooper.com. Remember to enter your favorite greeter from your store, church or business into "The Greeter Award" on my Web site.

I also do talks if you want to hear more!

See ya at The Store! Oh yeah... I hear there's a sale on batteries. ;-)

TWMA!

Mary Ellen Cooper